The Curious Solitude of Anise

a novel

Thea Swanson

Dorsett, McClaughlin and Whitney

DEDICATION

To John Farr, whose memory gave me George.

CONTENTS

Acknowledgments   i

Part I: Now and Then   1

2010   2

1983   8

Kitchen Visits   17

Valentine Luncheon   28

Part II: Lessons   33

At the Institute   34

In the World   46

Up the Ladder   68

Off the Ladder   72

Part III: Repairs   79

A Room of One   80

Homeless Vet #1   85

Homeless Vet #2   94

Cost of a Meal   107

Spring Banquet   114

Part IV: Rescues   123

The Last Taste   124

ACKNOWLEDGMENTS

I would like to thank Jan Priddy and Nick Kocz for their expert reads and advice; Nora Jacobson for her documentary, *Delivered Vacant*; Philly2Hoboken for his blog; and Will Nixon for his poetry, time and reflections on Hoboken.

PART I

NOW AND THEN

2010

Anise pushed her cart on the sidewalk, patchy with ice. Her body: mostly air and fabric, clutching heat and space. Her face: lined and weather-baked and forty-seven.

It was winter in Buffalo but clear, with crisp temperatures and no new snow for days. She took her time wheeling. She had brought her cart out because it was laundry day—the last Friday of the month, when it was quiet in the Laundromat, when all the college kids were in their apartments, when everyone was having fun or relaxing. She had luxuriated in the warmth of the Wash-and-Fold for two hours, washing and drying two loads, washing her hair in two minutes over the basin in the corner, away from the window, then mopping under her breasts and arms with a rag, her coat hanging open, concealing her public sponge-bath. Pulling a hot, threadbare towel out of the dryer, she had placed it on her wet head, closed her eyes, and sat on a hard, yellow chair.

Anise continued shuffling down Elmwood, deep in conversation with her invisible mother. "I know how to do it. I've been taking care of myself for years, no thanks to you." A bicyclist sped by on the sidewalk, startling her, and she stopped in her tracks, one hand on the cart, one on her heart. "Crazy people," she said, peering at the back of the cyclist as he shot off the sidewalk and swerved around a parked car and down the street, out of view.

With a gloved hand, she gripped the handle of the cart and continued back home, still shunning advice.

"How many times have I walked these icy streets?" Anise spoke to her left, always to her left. With each difficult year out in the elements, ideas came to her, connections made, blame to tack on to her mother who her father had all but canonized. But she was no saint, Anise had discovered, years ago.

"Ha!" Anise barked to her left, letting go of the cart with her right hand. And with that movement, her ankle twisted inward, and she crashed to the hard ground.

Anise lay there, whimpering, squeezing her eyes shut at the pain in her thigh where she landed. The cart lay on top of her. Mostly though, she whimpered because being helpless was what she hated most. She depended on no one; it was second nature—no, first nature. Anise panicked and squirmed under the cart, her heart-rate increasing. Then a hand was suddenly gripping her arm, and she froze and looked up.

"Can I help you?" A young man stood before her, a man in his twenties with dark hair and fair skin who lifted the cart off her.

"George?" Anise was breathy.

"Can you stand up?" He held out his arms and stood there, arms outreached, arms that could heal all her pains, she was sure. Anise locked her eyes into his and held out her arms as well, allowing herself to be lifted as high and as far as he wanted to take her.

Anise clutched him as he lifted her off the ice. For three seconds, she rested her cheek on his chest, eyes closed. It had been so long since she had any human touch, and a man's chivalry, a lifetime.

"Are you okay?" he asked.

"Yes," she said, not knowing what she was answering

to, but it seemed correct.

He released his hold while her arms hung in midair.

"You sure?"

She dislodged her stare, aware and ashamed. "Yes, yes. Thank you." Turning toward her cart, she was somewhat disappointed her feet worked fine.

"Okay, then. See ya'." He took off quickly, not mature enough to say something more appropriate.

The spell was broken.

Feeling more of a monster than before the fall, she brushed down her coat, gripped the handle of the cart and continued on home. A block more and she was there. Stopping on the sidewalk for a moment and looking up and down the street, she made sure no one was nearby. All was clear. She dragged her cart up a narrow driveway of the tiniest of boarded up storefronts. Once she got around to the back, she was safe. Dragging her cart up one cement step, she rested on the square of the landing. Then, with a key that no one knew she had, she turned an old lock and entered the building.

Anise pulled the cart over the threshold, one wheel at a time and wheeled it into the little backroom of the old restaurant. She didn't enter the restaurant proper but stayed in the anteroom. She had used this room on and off for years. A whole year had gone by without the latest owner popping by suddenly, showing the property to a potential buyer or checking the pipes. Early on in the year and many times before, Anise had been ready to escape, all belongings packed. But since last winter, not a soul had visited. Since summer, Anise had slowly made the spot her home.

Not a home as she would want it, but a piece of each main element was there: one book, candles, a cat, and most importantly, cooking supplies. The book would change as she would replace it at the Book Exchange up the street, accompanied by fifty cents. The candles she would use only to brighten her pages as she lay on old blankets that she kept folded during the day in a broom closet. The cat, well, the cat had been with her for thirteen years, was named Mandy after the mandarin orange, and was the one living thing that she could stroke with affection.

It was bright enough to prepare a decent dinner without stumbling in the dark. First, Anise took off her coat, still warm enough with the layers underneath, and she brightened with vigor for this part of the day. From a cupboard that she kept dust-free, she retrieved her homemade stove: two tuna cans—one big, one small. The cans were punched with holes, one placed inside the other. Fuel was isopropyl alcohol. From her cart, she removed items she had obtained early that morning from the food bank: an onion, and something precious that the volunteer had turned over in her hand three times.

"It's way past the due-date," she had said, about to discard it.

"No! Anise exclaimed, reaching to save its demise. "It's cheese. Good cheese. It doesn't go bad."

Softened by Anise's worried expression and her withdrawn hand that she held to her chest, the volunteer handed her the Emmental.

"It's against policy. It's so old. But since you want it so much." The woman placed it in a plastic bag.

"Do you have an onion?"

"Wouldn't you rather have some canned goods?" She was a new volunteer and didn't know Anise's ways.

"No, thank you." Anise had learned it was easier not to divulge, easier to let them think what they will.

The woman shrugged and walked back to the perishable aisle to retrieve an onion. She brought back three bananas, too, seeing that they were turning, and placed them in the bag.

"No, thank you," Anise said.

The woman looked at her with surprise and removed the bananas, handing Anise the bag. "Here you go," she all but hollered, ending with a sigh. "Have a good day," and she brushed away nothing on the counter, not looking at Anise, offended at her rejected offering.

Anise had brushed her away, too. The interaction was one of hundreds she experienced, from both ends of the spectrum. During the years, she had learned to detach from such interactions, be they contemptuous or compassionate. She had learned that the spectrum was much closer than one could know, that hate and love were side-by-side, that a person, like this woman who was there to help people, could in a moment of judgment, turn her back.

And now, back in her anteroom, Anise did not think about the woman. Instead, she reveled in her dinner-making, in the whole ingredients, in what she could do with them, how she could take an onion and cheese and make something wonderful.

Mandy felt her happiness and brushed up against her leg. And Mandy would get a portion.

"Yes, Mandy." Anise looked down at her old friend. "Dinner is good. No matter what, dinner is always good."

She set everything up before lighting the little stove, so as not to burn away precious fuel. A lidded-pot that contained all her cooking utensils and a few edibles, just a few things, but it was all she needed. First, she chopped onions into tiny squares. She kept a two-liter pop bottle of water that she'd refill from various sinks or spigots, and from this she poured water into a small pot. Three quarters of a stick of butter she still had, and this she set aside. After lighting her stove, she added the onions to the water. Her movements were quick and agile; she stirred, and then she chopped cheese. After a while, when the onions were barely there and translucent, and the water was more of a broth, she added a little salt. It was time for roux: butter in the pot and then flour whisked in. She had no scalded milk to add to make true Béchamel, and for a moment this saddened her, but no bother: She had the cheese, which she scooped with her hands into the pot, delighted.

6

When it was done, she placed Mandy's meal on the floor nearby, then she sat on her blankets that she had taken from the cupboard. She placed her bowl of sauce on her lap with bread in hand for dipping. It wasn't formal, but it was the best she could do. The bread was not good either, not baked by hand but by a machine somewhere with a thousand other loaves, but it was something. She dipped and tasted. It was good. She closed her eyes and chewed in the dim light that came from the small, high window. "Yes, Mandy. Good cheese is all we need." She chewed in the quiet—so quiet, she could clearly hear Mandy's soft noises. "Though dessert would be nice, don't you think?" Desserts had always been her favorite. And as she chewed, she remembered.

1983

Anise and George and numerous other Hutchinson Central Technical High-schoolers boarded the public bus, flashing their passes at the driver. Anise slid into a seat, then George next to her. Plunking their backpacks on their laps, they made the usual adjustments, George pulling down the back of his bomber jacket that rode up, and Anise pulling down her teased, blonde bangs over her right eye. Their back-home antics followed.

"Watch this," Anise whispered, retrieving a FORTRAN punched card from her Computer Science binder. She showed George what she had typed at the top of the card.

George opened his mouth, laughing without sound.

Anise watched the passenger who sat in front of her: a working woman going back home from a day in the office downtown. Anise examined women often—perplexities, all of them. What paths did they take to get to where they were? Did they live alone? Have children? What were their jobs, exactly? Jobs were very important to Anise. They spoke of direction, dedication, and longevity.

This woman's profile was more *together*—a word her mother would have used—than what Anise wanted.

Anise's shenanigans could backfire. A camel-colored wool coat, something her mother would have never worn—never had the money, and even if she had, Anise doubted she would have even thought of buying a coat like that. Bubble coats. That's what her mother had worn. Pink and gray.

Anise hesitated, pulling the card back down to her lap.

"Go on," George urged her with his elbow.

Anise waited until the woman looked away from the window. When she did, Anise carefully placed the card in the narrow window ledge and pushed it forward. The typed words read: "PLEASE REPORT TO THE FRONT OF THE BUS. THE DRIVER WOULD LIKE TO SPEAK WITH YOU."

The woman soon looked out the window and retrieved the card. Success! Her head was down as she read the mysterious text. Her confusion was almost too much to bear! Her freshly washed bob turned, and with it, her furrowed brow. Anise's victory plummeted, as did the sweat that trickled down her side, absorbed by her bra.

Anise and George assumed innocent faces, George's brown eyes examining the back of the person's head across the aisle, Anise's blue eyes intent on her own fingernails.

"Don't you kids have anything better to do?" The woman stared, not turning back around, but actually waiting for an answer.

George copped a puzzled face, knotted his brow, questioned with a cock of his head.

"Don't give me that." She twisted her body and sized-up Anise. "And I'd advise you to get that smirk off your face, or I'll just take your name and number and call your mother."

"My mother's dead."

"That explains it." The woman turned around.

The bus jerked to a stop. People got off, including the camel-coated, annoyed, together woman. Before exiting, she tossed a look their way: *grow up.*

"What a bitch!" George said quietly to Anise. His nose was shiny. Sparse black hairs poked over his top lip.

"We asked for it." Anise wanted to disappear. She loved the thrill of causing confusion, but she didn't like being caught. George was different. He didn't mind being caught. He would do anything to put on a show.

Anise and George got off the bus together, even though George had to walk two extra blocks. After walking a block, Anise stopped dead in her tracks, despite the wind and the snowflakes that were beginning to fall.

"George."

"Yeah?" It took him a minute to stop and shift his feet, turn around. Anise had noticed he had been gaining weight for the last two years, since his parents' divorce. It affected how he moved; everything about him seemed slower than before. Sometimes, Anise would watch him stare at nothing.

"I think you have a huge amount of potential." Anise's arms were stiff at her sides, her teased bangs blown back by the wind, and the rest of her blonde hair—too curly and too much, she had always thought—whipping around as the wind increased.

"So do you. C'mon, I'm cold." George thought she was putting on a show, but he wasn't up for it—his spirits would rise and fall in minutes—and people had to be around for the show. As George turned around, he saw no one, and he became uncomfortable and pulled down the elastic of his coat.

"No, George. I'm serious. You can do amazing things in life. Whatever you want." She started walking with him to relieve the agony that registered on his face. "What I mean is, don't let what people say stop you or bring you down."

"Who's been talking about me?" George smashed his fists in his jacket pockets.

"No one." Anise shoved her hands in the pockets of her surplus army jacket. "I just think you have a lot of talent, you know, with your drawing, and I'd hate to see that wasted."

They continued on in silence until Anise detoured onto Meridian Street.

"See ya' tomorrow, George."

"See ya'," George sounded miserable and worried, not waving his big, goofy goodbye like usual.

That's not what Anise intended. That's not what was supposed to happen. She had been reading *Make Everyone Think You're Wonderful* that she picked up from a self-help display at the Cazenovia Library and was encouraged to take the advice she was reading and offer it to those around her. She had been starting with herself, gazing in the mirror, peering at her image, searching for the good, the positive, the symmetry in the asymmetry of the lopsided smile she had been born with. Was she pleasing just the way she was? And really, what did anyone else's ideas of her matter anyway? Yet the book said self-confidence was the key to happiness, to success, and part of successful happiness was how her inner beauty would become outer beauty and how everyone would not be able to resist her simply because she thought she was irresistible and therefore radiated beautiful, happy, self-confident success. They would want to be her.

Anise was having a hard time bursting through with her own amazing potential—being shy in bigger groups, self-conscious—so she thought she'd start with others.

Her dad she bypassed—after all, this wasn't about making miracles, just a shift in perspective—and she had thought about the next person she could help: George. But it didn't work; George was left suspicious and worried, lumbering home in a heavy gate.

Anise pushed open the door of her small, neglected house, the screen door missing its spring and slamming behind her. She was alone, she knew, because it was 3:40 P.M. Her dad, Carl, didn't get home until he was done at the auto shop, 5:30 P.M. these days. It was good—he was good, right now. Predictable, at this point, slow and quiet, not like in the years right after her mother's death when he wouldn't come home from work, when Anise was left to fend for herself, turning the thermostat to seventy degrees when home from school, turning it down to fifty-five before bed, like she had seen her mother do. The mattress cold, she'd curl in her feet, tuck them close to her bottom, her nightie too thin, but no one to tell. The cold mattress was so saggy and old that she felt like she was being pulled down, drowning, like her mother had drowned.

The day that it happened, Laura, her mother, had kicked off her sandals and waded in Lake Erie when the three of them were having a picnic. She had been doing odd things lately, dying her hair, buying new clothes, snapping impatiently at Carl. The area she waded in wasn't open to swimmers, but she ignored Carl's pleas and an undertow pulled her in. Carl had barely been able to articulate words through sobs in the ambulance over the plastic-covered corpse. *Laura was so full of goodness...even the lake wants her.* Anise hadn't cared what the lake wanted or how good her mother was. She just wanted her mother back like before, not the heavy, cold thing that was lying next to her under plastic.

During those evenings and years in the house alone, at seven and eight years old, Anise came to accept that both her parents had left her. And with the leaving, though she couldn't articulate it, the safety and contentment that were actual, physical parts of Anise—like a heart, or a lung— had left, too. She hadn't been aware she had such things as safety and contentment until they were gone. But she learned she wasn't getting them back. She'd feel this way when making a dinner of toast, or when bringing home class pictures that her father would finally see a day late, creasing them with his shaky grip from a night out, never framing them.

Anise's childhood light had gone out.

On some days, right after the drowning, when Anise would come home from school, Carl would try hard to make up for not being home. Lanky, all arms and legs, moving quickly—though shakily—through the kitchen, he'd mash potatoes, sweat beading on his forehead, while Anise stood at the counter, watching vigilantly, needing the moment more than air, yet all the while knowing it was just as intangible. She'd smile her crooked smile and dip her finger in the creamy lumps, pained by the pain in his eyes, but knowing bravery was best.

But things were different now, and there was comfort in the rust on the screen, the mail that she flipped through—tearing out grocery coupons, opening the heat bill with a squint. She'd plan the monthly budget based on Dad's paychecks. She found comfort in the dinners she made. Often hamburgers, canned peas and fried potatoes, or baked chicken and boxed cornbread. She'd do this for the both of them, and she'd do it with ease, closing the refrigerator door with her hip. She'd tie back her hair and toss a dishtowel over her shoulder, peeling potatoes faster than her dad—and maybe even her mom—into the sink before sweeping them up with her fingers and into the trash.

Potential. It was making her antsy. This idea that people in themselves contained all that was necessary was eating at Anise. After kicking off her shoes and tossing her backpack on the bed, still thinking about George's potential, she headed to the kitchen, stood in the doorframe, and saw the room anew. *Even this kitchen.* Returning to her room, she unplugged her cassette player and brought it to the counter, placing it next to the electric can opener, which for the first time appalled yet inspired her. Red sauce was caked in the ridges of the cutting device; a brown sticky substance covered its lever. Soap! That's all it would take! It would look brand new; she was sure of it. She scanned the boomerang-patterned counter, all the many objects that could be cleaned, organized, thrown out. Then further around the kitchen—it was almost overwhelming—cobwebs, dirty curtains, a crock-pot on the floor, in the corner.

Hovering over her tape deck, she pulled out the cassette, turned it around and stuck it back in. After pressing the play button, she opened the cupboard below the sink, took out a bucket and blasted it with water while singing "Goody Two Shoes" with Adam Ant whose symmetrical and painted beauty hung on her bedroom wall, all tight, red leather and loose, white cotton, a five-foot poster that in the evening she desperately imagined was a two-way mirror as she danced to it, smoking a Marlboro she'd snag from her dad's pack while he watched TV on the couch.

But now in the kitchen, she didn't dance to Adam Ant. She opened cupboards, examined crevices. The cupboard above the sink, for instance, in the right corner, hugging the wall. Usually, she would open and close it in one motion, remembering no salt was there, no macaroni, no cocoa, just orphaned plastic containers missing lids, shoved there, claiming space for no reason, probably for years.

This was a new day, however. A time to examine, to inspect, to scrutinize. Strip that kitchen clear of clutter— that's what she wanted to do. Find the hidden potential in this brown and greasy place. It had been forgotten, hidden really—the real kitchen, under years of quick-washing the two-quart sauce pan, so that it could be used the next day.

Singing with Adam about exposed heartbreaks and putting makeup on the good side of one's face, she was sure the song was meant for her. In her element, she opened the far-right cupboard above the sink to clear it out.

Margarine containers. One stacked inside another, five, six of them, taking up the space of an entire cupboard. "What a waste," Anise said, pulling out the stack, three of them falling and bouncing off the counter and onto the floor. She was about to go after them when she noticed something else, a book of some sort, or a binder of old papers that had been pushed toward the back.

The book cover was red-gingham plaid. Anise's breath caught, and she had to sit down, right on the floor. She knew this cookbook. Its memory hit her like the margarine containers, tumbling down and smacking. Or like a forgotten image of her mother that every now and then splashed its colors suddenly, jiggled free by a related occurrence. And now this *Better Homes and Gardens* cookbook that boasted, "Every Recipe Tested in Better Homes & Gardens' Tasting-Test Kitchen." A chill shook her shoulders, quite unannounced. Then, a warmth, a pressing on her left shoulder, so that she turned to see.

Nothing.

The book looked smaller than she remembered. Smaller in her own hands, yet it had looked bigger in her mother's. How could that be? Could her hands now be bigger than her mother's had been?

Anise opened the book. Her chest rose and fell. The cover came completely off. On the inside of it, she read:

> *Sixteenth Printing of De Luxe Edition*
> *Copyright, 1941, 1942, 1943, 1944, 1945, 1946, 1947, 1948*

And under that, in faded ink:

> *To Laura,*
>
> *May your table contain as much love as my heart contains for you.*
>
> *Love,*
> *Mother*

Anise had one memory of her grandmother before she died, the only grandparent she ever knew, and it was simply this: a big, kitchen chair in a small, yellow kitchen and a gentle hand patting the spot. *Here, Anise. Sit here.*

Anise placed the book cover on the linoleum. She carefully turned the "Outstanding Features" page to the next page, which said that every morning at eight the Better Homes & Gardens staff was at work testing recipes that people from all around the country sent in. She wondered if they still did that, almost forty years later, if her mother ever sent in a recipe.

There were twenty tabs, the first labeled "Nutrition" and the last "Table Setting." Paging quickly through "Nutrition," she rested on tab two: "Meal-Planning and Meal-Making." It spoke of meals being fun games that bring applause and joy.

Anise turned more pages. Again and again she'd find a pen marking, an underlining, a star, a note, and the wonderful thing, the surprise, the unexpected, was that they seemed alive. The markings seemed freshly scrawled—though she knew they couldn't be, knew that they weren't. But they were *there*, little scratched guides in blue, written reminders that her mother did care. She cared so much that she wrote it down. She had intentions. She had intentions to use more butter than the recipe called for the next time she'd make it for her little family.

Anise closed the book. Held it to her chest, rolled on her back. *What a day!*

Kitchen Visits

Even a coffee bean has potential.

For the past two months, following her cookbook discovery, Anise found herself taking the bus to Blue Mountain Coffee on Elmwood on the west side of Buffalo every Monday instead of going straight home after school. She'd buy one pound to last the week. Maybe it would be Kona, Snicker-doodle, or Jamaica Blue. Maybe Sumatra or Viennese. Whatever flavor, she knew freeze-dried coffee would never enter her house again. Her father knew it too and had come to expect the good stuff since the first time she served it, when he lifted his eyelids, glassy through the aromatic steam, and said, "This is damn good coffee, Cookie." She smiled her crooked smile and both of them were hooked.

True, she started drinking coffee at sixteen, but there were worse things she could do.

This day, this Monday, she took George with her to Blue Mountain.

"Who cares about coffee?" George dragged his sneakered feet through the entrance. A customer looked their way.

"You know George, sometimes I feel like I don't even

know you." She squinted at him, shaking her head. "C'mon, over here." They walked to a display of shiny blue packages. Anise plucked *Chocolat Chocolat* from the glorious bunch and pressed it to his nose. "Smell."

"Does it taste like that?" His eyes widened.

"Yes."

"I'd rather just eat the chocolate. Saves me the work. Which reminds me, I'm hungry." He dropped his backpack to his feet and began to rummage.

"George, we need to talk." She stood a foot away, eyebrow lifted, hand on hip.

"Oh, no. Not again. I don't want to hear it." He clawed through his bag.

"Think of this coffee, George." She held the firm bundle directly in his line of sight. "Up until recently, my dad's been drinking *instant*." Her eyes were lasers of disgust. She placed the package back, just so.

"So?" He located the Juicy Fruit, unwrapped a stick while Anise watched, her mouth involuntarily watering.

"It's all related, George." Anise, as was her way lately, felt the need to convert, and spoke with intensity. "What we put in our bodies—even *how* we put it in."

"I put gum in my mouth, Anise. Slowly. Like this." He folded the soft stick into his mouth and chewed, eyes half-closed.

"Whatever." Anise stepped away from George and further into the store, seemingly discarding his indifference. She decided to look for a new flavor while she was at it, though *Chocolat Chocolat* was her favorite so far.

Blue Mountain was good for her in some respects. It got her out of the house, which she had been spending a lot of time in lately. Plus, she switched from smoking Marlboro (so full of additives), to all-natural Nat Sherman, their various flavors displayed like expensive truffles behind the counter that she stood at presently.

"May I have a pack of Fantasia, please?"

She couldn't resist the gold-tipped pastel sticks. And they were "lights," too, which made her feel better about the fact that her habit had picked up speed. She was up to five a day now.

"Okay, Miss health nut." George hung his puffy arm on the glass counter. "Explain."

"If I'm going to do it, I'm going to do it right."

They stepped out of the store and onto trendy Elmwood Avenue. Crossing the street and waiting for a bus, Anise unwrapped her Nat Sherman's. With her hand curved over a match, she blocked the mid-winter wind. After taking a drag, she blew out smoke and smiled at George who scowled.

Anise loved George in a way that was, as far as she could describe, indescribable. He wasn't like a brother, she didn't think, though she had no reference except that his devotion to her wasn't altogether brotherly, though he never came right out and said it. It was in his actions, big and small. He'd let her get on the bus first—though she had a sense it wasn't due to chivalry as much as wanting her Jordache-jeans at eye level. Not a brotherly desire, she didn't think. And they never argued; they only spent time together—unusual pastimes, entertaining themselves by embarking on strange dares. Like walking inside Mercy Hospital as if they were visitors, into the chapel there and flipping over the Persian rug that lined the apse. The more original the act of strange defiance, the more hilarious.

Imagining the eventual, confused reaction was half the fun. In the Seneca Mall, for instance. Serenely swooshing by, Anise would pull wigs down over the faces of mannequins. George would hang women's underwear from the graceful hands of the sporty males. Anise would swipe a toaster on display in Housewares and place it on a sofa in Furniture. Yes, physically placing something where it shouldn't be was the driving force behind most of their humor. The inherent contradiction, the oddity in the small gesture was funny enough.

Through all that silliness, there was an intimacy that, years later, Anise still wouldn't be able to define. *Two* years later, after George headed off for the Art Institute of Chicago, she received a card in the mail that curiously made mention of their future together: "…and when you visit I can show you the museum…" Visit? She hadn't thought of visiting. When people left Anise's life, she figured they were gone. Visiting was a wishy-washy, indefinable, temporary place that she'd rather not be a part of. She had tossed the card in the trash, discarding its incongruity, bothered by the loose connection, gone but not gone. Just go already!

But that day, that year, George was fully present, and she could count on him—often more than her dad. And as she smoked her Necco-pink Fantasia Light, she got a thrill at George's incredulity that she should smoke at all, let alone stand there and smoke in broad daylight, people and cars zipping by, the two of them standing in front of Mykonos restaurant, half-full of customers, a big glass window only five feet away.

"Oh, c'mon George, don't be mad at me. It's just once in a while. A girl's gotta live a little."

George looked away. It was that kind of gesture that she couldn't quite name, but if she were forced to, years later, she might have simply said, *he cared.*

But this day, Anise giggled in response. She was always being such a good girl, taking care of so many things. Where was her chance to claw a little back? Revolt? Why was it that everyone else could revolt but her? Dad revolted about once a month with his six-packs. So there. Anise's little revolution. A cigarette. Big deal.

George still wouldn't look her way, at her sullied aspect. Anise's guilt kicked in, and she put out the expensive cigarette on the bus-stop post to save for later. She inserted it in the fancy box, then in her jacket. Smoking put a chasm between the two of them. She was now, *different*. She definitely didn't want that, not now, not when she was realizing new things about life. About potential. About Beef Short-Rib Crown. About her sneaking suspicion that her mother was in the kitchen with her when she cooked.

"George." Anise waited for him to glance her way.

"I see the bus coming." George felt for change in his pocket. They were now outside the designated route, so the driver wouldn't take their passes.

"George, I lied to you the other day." She implored, not minding that the wind took her teased bangs out of her right eye.

"About what?" Things weren't feeling so great lately for George. He had been wishing things would straighten themselves out soon. It was bad enough having his mom change nursing shifts to second at the hospital. He'd been wandering through the quiet house when he got home, not happy to heat up leftovers, not really sure how. Now Anise was acting weird lately and lying to him.

"About why I didn't want to go to the movie last night. It wasn't because I was tired." She shifted her backpack. "It was because I wanted to make an orange fig whip."

The bus pulled up and opened its doors with the usual screech. They were so use to the sound that they continued to stare at each other in earnest until the driver interrupted.

"Hey kids, you coming?"

George got on first, a first in itself. He walked down the narrow aisle, choosing the seat—another first. He went clear to the back, passing right by an empty two-seater. Planting himself smack in the back center necessitated Anise to either sit crammed between him and a big kid who hung his leg partially over the empty seat, or to sit in a seat adjacent to George, facing the aisle. She chose the latter, feeling a little indignant. He was definitely overreacting.

For a few stops, she let the usual adolescent discomfort

21

of across-the-aisle bus etiquette guide her. That meant she didn't converse with her best friend and pretty much acted as if they weren't together. She looked out the window, the facades passing quickly before her. Casa di Pizza, The Community Music School, large Victorian homes now cut up into offices and apartments. This is where she longed to be. In this part of Buffalo. The Elmwood Strip. At night, blue lights lined the tops of the businesses. This she knew because when she graduated from eighth grade, dinner at Casa di Pizza was the celebration. It was the first time she had gone out to dinner. Dad was cleaner than she could remember him ever being, the rims of his ears shiny, the usual car oil in his fingernails scrubbed almost completely away with Lava soap. Her light-blue dress was airy as she walked on the stage—too airy because Dad didn't know about such things as slips, and Anise hadn't figured that one out yet. But it didn't matter because she graduated top of the class, and he beamed, standing up in the audience, whistling. He cried too, at the restaurant, but he held her hand, which made it okay. The light was dim and every table had its own lamp that for some reason Anise knew to think the word, *Tiffany*. And her own menu. And ordering such a thing as carbonara style pasta. And the folded fifteen-year-old newspaper article that Dad removed from his shirt pocket and smoothed on the table.

"Do you see her there?" Pointing to a woman in the grainy photo, Dad's voice was urgent as he unveiled the relic, the sacred text. In the picture, Laura stood between two of many long tables, setting down a platter of food between two coated men. The article was titled, "Carmelites Serve Needy at Salvation Army Dinner." It had been Christmas Day, the article said. Anise read the piece twice, grasping at the truncated flow of journalistic prose.

"What's a novice? A helper?"

"No, Cookie. Your mom was going to be a nun until I swept her off her feet." He took a sip of water from the

22

cold glass on the table. "I thought you should know. Now seemed a good time." He searched his coat for his Marlboros. "Your mom was a special lady, Anise, and I'm not just saying that because I'm her husband and because I'll always be her husband." He pushed his hand through his graying hair. "I'm saying that your mom was the most giving person I ever met. This photo is just one example. She was *always* feeding people, helping the poor. She turned my life around, Anise. And when she wasn't helping people, she was thinking about it. If she had one fault, I guess that'd be it." He lit his cigarette, took a drag. "She was never satisfied, it seemed. She might be next to us on the couch, watching TV, but her mind was someplace else. You could see it in the wiggle of her toes. She went out of her way, *looked* for opportunities. It was *you* that kept her home. She was actually *happy* changing your diapers." He shook his head.

Their salads came. Mom may have been happy, but now Anise wasn't. She rested her cheek in her hand, played with her fork, felt like a third wheel to all of this. Mom had other desires—God, helping hundreds—maybe thousands—and Dad.

"So, you were a bum when you met mom?" Anise knew that was mean, but she let it come out.

"I wasn't on the street—yet. But I was on my way." Her dad always gave it to her straight, and for that, she was thankful.

"So what did you do that was so wonderful that made her want to give up being a nun?"

The lamplight sparkled in his watery eyes. "I said, 'Thank you for the ham, m'aam. Will you marry me?'"

The big kid lifted his weighty leg off the bus seat and landed it in the aisle proper, stood, and lumbered to the doors. As the doors folded open, he looked at Anise and George. "Sayonara," he said and stomped hard down the steps, his grand exit.

A fine opportunity for joint laughter, for sure—the unexpected—yet when Anise landed her amused gaze on George, he was unmoved.

"Why are you so mad?" Anise held her backpack tight.

"You lied to me." George stared straight ahead. "You could have just told me you wanted to make an orange whip. I'm not stupid. I would have understood." Though he didn't understand how making a whip was better than going to the movies.

"It's an orange *fig* whip and I don't think you're stupid." She bit her thumbnail. "It's not just the cooking."

"Cooking?" George had thought weaponry.

"It's other things, too." Anise changed seats, sat next to George. Taking a deep breath and exhaling, she questioned her best friend. "Promise you won't take off on me?"

"What do you mean?"

"Promise you'll be my friend, and you won't think I'm crazy."

"Why would I think that?" George didn't think cooking was all that good a reason to miss a movie, but it was a perfectly normal activity. Plus, lately he had been wishing he knew how to cook.

"When I cook, I have these…feelings." Anise closed her eyes.

George understood having feelings about food.

Since his dad and mom divorced, George had feelings about food. Feelings of filling up that empty space Dad put there when he took his shirts and shaving cream and mitt. His mitt, while George's mitt remained. Still remains, unused, unfilled, no ball smacking the leather, filling the palm. Filling space—food did this well.

"Why didn't you just tell me?" George finally looked at Anise, the bus's bounce hurting. He felt a little sick.

"I was afraid you'd think I was weird." Anise adjusted her bangs.

"I wish you'd give me some credit sometimes." George took on a new demeanor, one that keeps wisdom and mystery in deep recesses. "There's a lot about me you don't know."

"Oh, we missed our stop!" Anise jumped up and pushed the rubber strip to signal the driver. They scrambled to the door and bounded off the bus and into downtown Buffalo. They walked back a couple blocks to get to their transfer stop, the number fourteen bus to South Buffalo.

As lofty as George seemed, Anise knew he still didn't get it. "George. Here it is." She halted before reaching their stop at Mohawk and Washington. "My mom has been visiting me, I think."

"I thought she was dead?"

"She is."

He exhaled, tolerating this mumbo-jumbo. "Explain what this has to do with food."

"She visits me when I cook. Kind of directs me." Anise began walking again and tossed her hands in the air. "I don't know, maybe I'm crazy."

George caught up with her. "So invite me over. I'd like to meet her."

She scowled. Walked faster.

He walked faster too.

"I don't think you're lying," said George. "Maybe just…mistaken."

Anise stopped.

"Do cookbook pages turn on their own? Is that a *mistake*?"

He thought. "Wind turns pages."

"There was no wind, George. We don't open our windows."

"You probably turned the page and forgot."

"I felt a hand on my shoulder."

"A twitch. I get them all the time."

"I heard a soft voice."

"Someone outside, walking by."

"I started crying for no reason."

"I do that, too."

Anise gave it to him straight. "I was about to preheat the oven and it was already preheated. I went to grab a towel out of the drawer but it was folded on the table."

"You probably just forgot you did those things."

"I smelled her, George. I smelled my mother!" Anise placed her hand over her mouth and ran to the wall of a parking garage.

George followed.

"It's her skin. I remember the smell." Anise panted. "Explain that."

George leaned on the wall and said nothing.

They stared at the pavement for a minute. George dropped his backpack to his feet. Two pigeons waddled by, pecking at invisible food.

Anise sat on the cement and buried her face in her arms.

George remained standing as she whimpered.

Standing and silent.

Minutes passed, and her sobbing slowed.

Still, he said no word.

How did he know this was just what she needed? She needed George standing right there, right then, simply waiting. Anise looked up into the silence. George was real, and he was there, and he'd stand there as long as she needed. Forever maybe. Yes, George would stand there forever. Anise gaped. George remained. And when George knew it was safe, when Anise took the last of her big, slow breaths, sitting on the ground against the wall, he pursed his lips, a stern mouth, causing Anise to sputter a weak hint of a laugh.

"Stop, George. Not now," she pleaded, not wanting to laugh, wanting to hold on to the pain a bit longer. But there he was, his mouth puckered with feigned disdain, stepping into character. And then a pedestrian—bingo!

Perfect! He gave his all. The show of shows, all for Anise this time. All for Anise.

"Delores! Get up, Delores," George demanded.

But the last "Delores" came out with a laugh, and the stranger shook his head and tsk-tsk'd them, which made Anise giggle.

"Delores!" George gesticulated, pointing, as yet another person strode by. "Home to take your pills, Delores! Get up! Home!"

Oh, George. This. Let's hold onto this forever.

Audience gone, they both quieted. Straining to see George's expression, a sun ray shone in Anise's eyes, blinding her for a moment until she blocked it with her hand. Yes, he was there. Holding out her other hand, she waited for his.

Valentine Luncheon

George flipped his Police cassette tape over and pressed play. He cranked "Every Little Thing She Does Is Magic" and sang to it, his brush a microphone, sweat beading at his temples after just one and a half minutes. The song ended, and he hit the rewind button while he continued to get ready to see Anise, which included air drumming, which in turn triggered sweat under his arms: He had forgotten to put on antiperspirant. Grabbing his roll-on, he stuck it under his t-shirt and glided the ball until his arms and ribs were sticky and wet. He flapped his arms like a chicken to speed the drying. He looked in the mirror, happy with his Flock of Seagulls t-shirt that Anise liked but that he didn't. He had only bought it to impress her. She was getting more and more into weird music that he just didn't get. Shriekback, X, The Violent Femmes. They went places he didn't understand. He didn't want to go to places he didn't understand. Places like that were unstable. A person could flop. Could fail. Could be laughed at. No one laughed at The Police.

Valentine's Day. Perfect. Saturday, too. She said they had "special" things to cook. Yesterday after school, he stayed downtown, told Anise he was meeting his mom for a doctor appointment and that she should continue on home. At AM&A's there was a huge display of candies and gifts. He purchased three items: one red bear, one heart box, one pink card. When he got home, he spent thirty minutes drafting a poem on scrap paper. Originally fifty words that expanded into three paragraphs about how perfect they were for each other, the final version was eleven words total:

> *One bear, red*
> *One heart, red*
> *One George, red (for you).*

This day, he read his card again and tucked it back in the envelope. On his way through the large and drafty house, he stopped at the kitchen table and scratched a quick note to his mom who was out shopping before her evening shift. *Mom, Went to Anise's. Be back in a few hours. I took out the trash like you asked. George.*

George tucked his gifts in his jacket and headed out the side door of his brick house and down McKinley Parkway.

The road was one of the wider ones in the residential parts of South Buffalo, with two clearly marked lanes as well as room for parking on both sides. The sidewalks were clean, flat and bare. A tree grew here and there tucked near a home, but none grew next to the curbs, so George often felt vulnerable in the open space. And as he galumphed down his empty street and then made his way to narrow Meridian Street, he felt at ease with the squeeze of the block, the Maples near the streets that had buckled the sidewalks, the graying tarmac and homes with lives on display: bicycles on lawns, a neighborhood watch-sign on the corner. He approached Anise's house.

"My latest victim. Please enter at your own risk." Anise moved aside for George to enter her kitchen.

"You mean there have been others?" George held his jacket over his arm and presents.

Anise closed the door and assumed a Dracula dialect,

"Today, we suck blood." Then she spoke normally. "Or at least, chill loganberry juice." She smoothed down her gingham apron she haphazardly made from old curtains that skirted out over her Sex Pistols t-shirt. She linked her arm through his, leading the way to the counter.

George looked at the orderliness, the measuring cups and spoons, the bowls, bottles and packages. Red things. He placed his jacket carefully over his gifts and set them in one of the chairs.

"Ready, George?" she handed him an apron exactly like hers. "Lunch is not dinner, not as formal, but still, you want to show you care." George watched her profile as she pushed her veil of bangs behind her ear to get down to business. How he loved when her defenses were down. She smoothed the cookbook as if it contained the answers to everything. The dip of her lower lip was moist as she spoke.

"George, are you listening?"

"Hmm? Yes, yes. Beets." He wrapped the apron around his waist and was bewildered by his domestic transformation.

"C'mon, George, are you with me or not?"

"I'm with you. I'm with you." He bent toward the cookbook and read the recipe while smelling her forearm, so close to softness surrounded by bangles. He focused on the words on the page. "What are almond meats?"

"Think of it this way." She blew hair out of her eye with an upward blow while she measured long-cooking rice. "What's *meat*? It's the stuff inside a carcass—cow, pig, right? Well, *nut* meats are what's inside a nut carcass. Got it?"

"I never thought nuts were gross until now. Thanks." George held his stomach, then fingered the ruffle at the bottom of his apron.

"Stop being a wimp, George. If everyone thought for a moment where their food came from, they wouldn't eat it. Now, unwrap these bouillon cubes."

As George fumbled with the tiny squares, Anise's movements were quick and methodical. She set up cooking stations on the counter for each item of the Valentine luncheon. George gaped at her intensity over mushrooms and flour. The strawberries and candy hearts he could appreciate, but cornstarch? More of a mystery was how she knew what to do with all of it.

"So the cookbook lays it all out, huh?"

"Usually." Anise scooped flour with a measuring cup. "Sometimes I don't know what a word means, like, 'blanch,' or 'parboil,' but then I go to the glossary." She faced George. "You know what I love?" Her eyes were soft-blue lasers. "Making something from nothing. What's a pie? Separate ingredients scattered throughout the kitchen, just waiting to be something. It's up to me to make it happen." She unlocked her gaze from his. George blinked, the trance broken.

"Okay, Julia Childs." He picked up a spatula and wooden spoon and drummed on the counter. "Let's make magic."

Three hours later, the kitchen loaded with sticky bowls and pots, Anise and George dusty with flour, they placed a final plate on the table: a platter of Queen-of-Heart Tarts. George had to agree. It was something—similar to the drawing process where he took charcoal and paper into his room and hours later opened his door with images that would make his mother cry. He understood Anise's desire and felt it was just one more way they were alike. Cloverleaf rolls and almond sauce from flour and nuts. He was exhausted, famished. She was beautiful, glowing, placing little cards on the table. All this trouble she had taken for just the two of them, for a meal that would only be eaten and destroyed. He was beginning to understand the power of selflessness. The power of cooking.

The screen door slammed.

"Dad's here!" Anise yelped, glancing at the clock,

about to place a third card on the table. "Stay there. No, wait, come here! Stand behind your chair." Anise grabbed George's jacket from her dad's chair and tossed it to George. A bear, a card and a heart box tumbled to the floor. Heavy footsteps sounded in the hall. Anise blinked at the floor, then at George, whose face was pained. The doorknob turned.

The walk home was cold. The narrow street smothered him and the wide street drowned him. The bear and the heart and the card were crushed against his stomach, inside his jacket. He had quickly scooped them up as Anise escorted her dad to his seat. She never mentioned them, not through the beet-and-egg salad, not through the *Chocolat Chocolat*, not through the candy heart mints. Her eyes shined as she scooped rice with mushroom almond sauce onto her father's plate, letting George fend for himself. When her dad smiled upon tasting, she actually clapped. Why did she even bother to invite him? To be her helper? One thing he knew he wouldn't do: tell her he felt it. He had felt a cool tousle of his hair, but no one was there. Anise had startled at a tickle on her waist that she poked him for, thinking it was him. He'd die before he'd tell her. Let her suffer like he suffered.

Walking up his driveway, he stopped at his garbage can alongside his house, lifted the snow-covered lid and smashed the bear, heart and card on top of a smelly bag of tuna cans, toilet paper and macaroni-and-cheese gone bad.

PART II

LESSONS

At the Institute

It was at cooking school that Anise learned that a baker is not a cook; a pastry chef is not a chef. For a baker, there was the rising, the waiting, the urging along with an almost sixth sense. A baker had a relationship with the air. A baker could conjure yeast from the very substance she breathed. The bread was already there, waiting to live.

Much different from a cook, in the massive kitchens as she stood in her stiff, white uniform next to her fellow students. Cooks thrived in fast stress, in fast heat. The goal *was* stress and heat—you were supposed to *want* it, or at least, to want to want it. Heat from the stove, from the instructor, from the customers, from the clock. A never-ending fire. One could sear chicken forever and ever.

She needed time.

While some students had checked the clock continuously while they kneaded, Anise could knead forever, popping air bubbles under the heels of her hands, amazed that the dough—this basic necessity of life (or so it seemed to her)—that *she* created, responded. It was a love affair. Pressing hardness to softness. The dough would spread, would give, would expand and contract in rhythm. Anise would catch her breath when the timer buzzed, sometimes in a hiccup.

This was her great love. There would be no other.

Anise liked to be in the kitchen alone—this too, she discovered at the institute. Yes, the dishwasher was vital, and the line cook too, and everyone was needed in those huge kitchens to feed all those people—the entire school had to be fed lunch every day! But Anise didn't like the production-line feel of mass cooking, felt it took away from the integrity of doing it all with two hands—like she did in her kitchen on Meridian with her cookbook, maybe George by her side. But there was something else, too: Anise had had a suspicion that she was one of those people who would always feel at odds with humanity—it was a realization, really, a sudden realization. For days, she had stared in wonder across the enormous kitchen at Felice who was at peace in her skin no matter the company. *Charming,* she remembered writing in a letter to her dad that first semester she was away, when she was homesick. With an open, lipsticked smile, Felice looked like a maraschino cherry in her uniform, happy and plump in her own sticky sweetness, her dark curls poking out of her toque. And it had been such a shock, such an awakening to Anise, when on Felice's birthday, her four brothers, dark in the brow and white in the teeth, had burst into the kitchen, scooped up their sister who shrieked, and carried her clear through the swinging doors, her laughter and squeals echoing down the hall. The class had halted and then ran to see the finale through the high window: a giant cake—a chef's hat—on top of the family car. Anise bee-lined to the restroom where she shivered in a stall, inhaled deep breaths, and grasped her arms, trying to sort out her emotions. These she was able to sort out somewhat that night, writing to her dad. In lieu of sending the letter, though, she tore the hasty cursive in strips and burned each line with a cigarette, reading them as they vanished, *I guess it was the brothers, so many of them, loving her, knowing her, and....* It was during this ceremony that she concluded that people were the way they were for reasons they could do nothing about. Felice had obviously been surrounded by oodles of attention and care, so was her destiny. Anise brought these thoughts to a close by reasoning that she was like a hedgehog: solitary, nocturnal, prickly, groomed to being so. She'd accept attention, maybe even need it, but it was her nature, her inheritance, to pull into herself, letting her quills surround her, if for no other reason than because of the instinct to protect.

In the letter to her father that she burned, there were other words, too—secrets. Her confessions flew out, words about visits from her dead mom, about the guidance she received in the kitchen, but more than that, the hard secret, the secret that would destroy him, she was sure, the secret that fractured her own dreams.

The secret became her secret the day before Anise had left for culinary school. She was wistful about leaving her home, so she wanted to say goodbye. She walked through the house, lightly touching stationary items—the TV that Carl always watched, her posters on her bedroom wall. The kitchen she was going to save for last, because Anise felt Laura's presence only there.

Frightened that once she left Buffalo, the gentle touch of her mother would be gone, she wanted to see if there was something more she could take with her, something in addition to the cookbook, something more intimate.

She had gone into her dad's room. He had never gotten rid of his wife's belongings—this, Anise was used to. Her clothes were still in her dresser, and her brush and perfume were still on top, as if she had never died. Laura might walk in one day, sit down on her side of the bed, and brush her hair.

Anise had grown up with this stuck-in-time room, which seemed perfectly normal. Sitting on the edge of her parents' bed, Anise looked on the dresser-top, and though the brush seemed the right thing to take as it still contained her mother's hair, and Anise had memories of her mother brushing her own hair with it, she couldn't take it from what seemed a shrine and risk her dad noticing its absence.

Instead, Anise began to open drawers, something she had done many times when she was younger, but only the top two drawers that contained interesting things, such as a lint brush, letter paper, birth certificates, a broken watch Carl had gotten Laura years ago. But nothing seemed right to take. Really, most things seemed disposable, and that thought that gave her a pang of guilt because maybe she didn't care about the items now that she was off to something new.

She opened and closed the middle two drawers, which contained shirts and sweaters. She opened and closed the left bottom drawer quickly, bored with its contents—more dull sweaters—and right before she was ready to close the bottom right drawer, she plunged her hand under a tight stack of pants, touched an object, and withdrew a rubber-banded bundle of papers. The bundle was clearly a collection of handwritten letters that she assumed must have been written by her dad. Not interested in looking into their personal love-world, she shoved it back under the pants and closed the drawer. But once she closed it tight and stood, she thought it odd that a bundle of letters from her dad would be hidden, not just saved in the top drawer with other mementoes. Also, the handwriting was not familiar.

Sitting back on the bed, she yanked open the drawer, grabbed the letters, and with a heart that began to pound too hard because she was sneaking and because she was afraid of what she would find, she popped off the rubber band and carefully opened a letter.

The man wrote of Laura's soft skin and of her lips on his neck. He pined for her and couldn't wait to see her again. The letter was dated March, 1971. He signed it, "Missing You, Fred." Anise had been six years' old. Sweat rose on the back of Anise's neck. Her legs wobbled while she dropped the letter. She held the pile, closed the drawer with one hand, picked up the letter and left the room, marching down the hall. In the kitchen, she looked around for the answer. It was on the stove. A pan of brandy, ready to be the flambé for Cherries Jubilee, a special dessert to go with Steak Diane, one last special meal for Anise and Carl before she left to start her life.

She warmed the brandy. If it got too hot, it would boil the alcohol away. She had to be careful, but it was hard because her vision was foggy from tears and her hands shook as she opened letters without reading more of the offensive script, smoothed them out on the table, and then tore them into halves and thirds. She walked to the stove; the brandy seemed warm enough to ignite now. Turning off the burner, she piled the dry, loose paper on top of the brandy, lit a match, and tossed it on the mound. Flames flew up, catching the paper, some pieces burning quickly and floating in the hot air. Anise realized she had been remiss in taking precautionary steps. She should have been holding a lid in one hand to extinguish, just in case. She should have turned off the burner, too.

For two years, Anise had cooked in this kitchen, growing closer to her mother—not every day, but often enough. Her mother would come to her—or so she thought—and hum next to her, and blow in her ear to remind her to turn the oven down 100 degrees for the last half hour, and kick-start the hand-mixer when it would suddenly shut off when overheated. She'd even chop almonds for her—though Anise never actually saw it.

But now she started to doubt everything, wondered—as the image of her mother's lips on an old, ugly stranger's neck filled her head and made her wince—if she had imagined that her mother every really did visit her.

From the cupboard over the sink, Anise pulled out the cookbook. She squeezed it, stared hard at it, ready to turn it into flames, too—but she couldn't. She whimpered and dropped to the floor, shaking and chanting through her sobbing, *Please, please*, which really meant, *Is there anything I can believe in? Is there anything I can believe in?* After two minutes, she got up off the floor, opened the cupboard and jammed the cookbook inside. "Don't follow me. I've been fine without you all this time. You don't really care about me or dad. Just leave me alone." She slammed the cupboard door.

When her dad came home from work, Anise had the kitchen cleaned up, her food preparations in the garbage can on the side of the house, including her Filet Mignon, on the way to being Steak Diane.

"Hey, Cookie," Carl said, surprised at the sight of Anise in the living room.

"Hi, Dad." Anise said from the couch, lying like Carl usually did, face toward the TV, back flat. "Can we just go out for Texas Hots tonight? I have a big day tomorrow."

"Sure, Cookie," he said. "Let me just wash up."

"Thanks," Anise rolled on her side. She detected appreciation from her dad. She detected, in the lilt of his "sure," that it made him happy, if only for an hour, to be able to ease the pain of another and not have to face his own. She wondered if her years of picking up the slack was bad for him, after all. She closed her eyes and cried one more tear and wondered what else she may have been mistaken about.

****

Living away from home, Anise was prudent. Life had taught her well. While her schoolmates and coworkers bought new clothes, Anise shopped at thrift stores. Every extra dollar she squeezed in her hand, walked it to the registrar's office, slid it across the counter, and applied it toward her tuition.

There had always been a touch of that about her, of someone beyond her years. And she *had* been beyond her years, had been forced to be beyond her years in many regards. But if there was one area where she was still immature, where she would never fully mature, it was in the area of romance.

In the second semester of cooking school, Anise had her one and only experience with sex. Dean showed up as quickly as he would later vanish, leaving mid-semester, mid-day, without a word to anyone, not even the Registrar. But while he was there, he chopped celery across from Anise. He enticed her with his blue eyes shaded by black eyelashes. Adam Ant, there, in cooking school. Shorter than Adam, she assumed, and minus the makeup, but his fitted chef's jacket with its double row of buttons was close enough to the Napoleon costume. A black wave of hair hung over his forehead, and he'd often glisten, beads of sweat over his lip. Dean would move quickly, eyes like lasers on the fennel bulb, the shallots. A fast knife, he'd cut himself and suck his finger while Anise gaped, her ears hot. He'd take risks, like holding a carrot to peel instead of keeping it on the cutting board with his fingers to spin for speed. Chef DuBois would suddenly appear behind Dean, barking directions down the side of his cheek, intending to startle and call the careless soldier to attention, tell him of his wasted time, *waving your carrot like a haphazard conductor!* Anise would try to read Dean's reaction—Dean, who had clearly grinned at her more than once, was...shy? Coy? She sliced away her confusion, while Dean scanned the fit physique of the retreating chef, taking a breath and repositioning his carrot.

Dating experience would have helped Anise discern, but she didn't have any. George didn't count, of course. But she had no gauge, nothing but loneliness to measure Dean against, and when he knocked on her dorm-room door and asked if she wanted to go dancing, the loneliness vanished.

They drove in his old blue Pinto, given to him, she was told on the way, by his mother when he graduated high school.

"It was hers," he said, flicking ashes out the window as

they made their way around the river to the club, *Premier*. "She died three days after." He glanced her way. "Here she is." Reaching up to the rearview mirror, he stroked a black braid. Anise noticed it was streaked with white.

"Weird, isn't it?" said Anise. "How moms can die but still be around." Anise scanned the dash and the dark space around her feet, sure she'd see another fragment of Dean's mother clenching her son's earthly realm.

"Sounds like you've been through this." He peered at her, exhaled.

"I'm still in it." Anise motioned with two fingers for a drag.

Though Anise wasn't drinking age, the bouncer knew Dean and waved them both in. The bar was big and plain for the most part, very dark. Anise hadn't been in a club before—though she had walked by bars as a child and was familiar with them in a way once-removed, in the name mentioned by her father as he told her where he'd be if she needed to get a hold of him, or in the smell that wafted out of the heavy doors that shadowy men in faded jeans entered.

But this club was different. Dean shepherded Anise, his hand at the small of her back, and she blinked and sunk into the nurturing and attentive manner he assumed after their ride. He knew his way around the club, and he was gallant, telling her where the restrooms were, pointing to the empty dance cages that would be filled later with writhing individuals. She shook her head at such a notion.

"What can I get you?" Dean leaned against the solid edge of the bar, his royal blue shirt crinkling at his elbow.

No one had ever asked her that before, and she stumbled over words.

"Don't worry. I know people here." He motioned with his chin to the sinewy bartender at the other end.

Anise hadn't drunk in public before; in fact, it went against her nature, which was fashioned on making order out of disorder, and though she had sneaked some of Carl's beer not so very long ago, she had boarded up that tendency as quickly as it came when she felt the loss of control.

"I think I'll just have a Coke." Anise adjusted the small purse that strung across her chest and rested on her hip.

"Goody-two-shoes," he said. "C'mon, Anise, let loose. You're so stiff."

"Stiff?" Anise looked at her reflection in the mirror behind the bar: Curly hair tamed these days by a haircut above her shoulders and a tweed blazer she had bought with George at the Salvation Army to go against the grain at high school. Now it appeared humorless.

The bartender arrived. "What can I get you?"

"A gin and tonic," Dean looked at Anise, "and a—"

"Two gin and tonics, please."

Anise sipped her bubbly drink through the stirrer as she assessed the shapes and colors of the dark room that seemed to shift. She hadn't eaten dinner, so the gin moved quickly through her bloodstream. People were coming in the club in twos and threes now, a line forming at the door, and the room that had at first seemed warehouse-like was flashing. White shirts glowed against the black, and neon lights were luminous on the walls, pulsating with the music. And when one song disappeared into the next song that Anise knew well, spun by the DJ in the pillar on the floor, the same song she had played again and again on her boom box back in her bedroom on Meridian, and because the gin gave her the gumption, and the darkness was a shroud of protection, and the beat wouldn't let go, Anise had an idea. And when she saw Dean caressing his own chest as he batted his eyes at the bartender, and she felt the pang of betrayal, and when she saw the dance floor full of people, Anise had to let go, and she braced to seize the moment before it was gone, about to dance for the very first time in public, the last night in her life that she'd dance, and knowing it was now or never, she set her plastic glass on a little black table and placed one black shoe-boot on the dance floor and then thrashed like she had done a hundred times in her bedroom, but this time she was happy that she was surrounded by people.

Dean appeared before her, cool, dry, astonished.

"I had no idea!" he yelled in her ear.

"About what?" Anise pretended not to know.

"About you."

Another drink and Dean said, "Let's go."

"Already?"

"To another place. More intimate."

Anise shrugged and followed.

They drove to *Rio,* a much smaller bar, not far from *Premier. Rio* resided on a shabby, short block, sandwiched between a tax preparation office and a travel agency, which worked out perfectly: The offices were closed at night and the bar was closed at day. In the daylight, *Rio* was unnoticed: a darkened door and window, and the name of the establishment was forged in metal, small and discreet. In the wee hours, the three letters were backlit, illuminated for the people of the night: the ones who were desperate, the ones who were lost, the ones who led double lives.

"How do you find these places?" Anise asked as she closed the car door.

"They find me."

Inside, Anise's senses were slammed. Techno rhythms saturated the smoky space. Shoulders grazed, snaking through the narrow room. Genders overlapped, some transitions temporary, with makeup painted over dark pigments, and some transitions on their way to permanence, with breast buds proudly displayed in stretchy leotards, scoop necklines showcasing smooth skin belied by square shoulders and large hands.

Dean squeezed his way to the bar. Anise watched as he ogled a blonde boy next to him. She let the gin help her detach. Her head swam, and there were other things and people to keep her preoccupied. The DJ booth was raised, yet again. From what Anise could make out in the dark and through the bodies, the back room broadened into a dance floor. She detected bobbing heads.

Dean found her in the back, dancing in her own world. He handed her a glass. Anise took a big gulp.

"My, my. Things have changed." Dean was amused. "I knew you had a wild side."

"Oh really?" Anise tossed her hair back. "How could you tell?"

"You're here, aren't you?" He kissed her cheek, which stirred nothing in Anise. "You just needed the opportunity to let it out. I take full responsibility for your depravity."

Anise laughed and downed the gin. He was cute, but pompous. And wrong. It wasn't his doing. She was always in control of her life—she was sure of it.

"Thanks for being an equal opportunity—employer? Supplier? Something like that," she yelled near his face and handed him the empty glass, dizzy now.

Anise stopped dancing and sat on a painted bench near the dance floor. She couldn't focus anymore and gripped the edge of the bench, staring at the floor. Dean led her out of *Rio* and drove to his room. At the door, Anise fluctuated between laughing and telling him she had to go. He guided her teetering physique to his bed where she collapsed on rumpled sheets that smelled like him. Through half-closed eyes, she giggled at his concentration. During these seconds and minutes, Anise thought she was in command. Her heart told her head that because he couldn't get to her heart, she was the victor. But what her head didn't realize was that the very last thing he wanted was her heart.

He peeled off her leggings as she lay there, and any desire she might have had was squelched by the curious way he methodically removed her shirt without a sound and gestured with his hand for her to remove her bra.

When he removed his clothes, the gulf widened. He

44

stood over her for a moment with a grin, as if he was the gift. But this slight body that loomed was alien to Anise, a light-year away, with its unrecognizable terrain that seemed to contain no tenderness, nothing to call home, and she suddenly wished she could grab her clothes and go.

But he was on top without a word. With one hand, he pushed up one of her knees, and with other, he parted her legs. Without warning, they were joined. Two minutes later, without warning again, they were separate, and he reached over her to get cigarettes from his shirt on the floor.

Anise blinked at the ceiling. She reached down to the floor, clawing for something she had lost.

On Monday, she stood with her classmates at the counter in the large kitchen. A tall toque rested on her head, tilted like a dunce cap. With a mortar and pestle, she ground fresh garlic to a pulp. "Excellent," Chef DuBois remarked. "Class! Come see. Learn from Anise how to grind!"

In the World

The world, Anise had discovered, was full of baked goods. Endless, like a continuous line of stars that circled Earth, a flaky or eggy or dense or light or sweet or savory or filled or fried star, a continuous constellation, the *pastromeda*, perhaps. The more she learned about baking, the more she realized she could never learn it all. At some point in time or place, in century or country, in French *pâtisserie* or Beijing kitchen, she'd have to just slam the cookbook shut and say, *that's enough*.

Anise didn't travel the world to learn this—just Hoboken to Manhattan. After graduating, Anise answered two ads that hung on the student bulletin board: a room on Bloomfield Street in Hoboken and a bakery chef assistant in the West Village. The pay wasn't good, but that didn't matter because the room was $350 a month. What mattered was baking and carving out a life of her own. She had heard that to make it in New York City you just had to have determination. Persistence was more important than talent. She had both. And she thought she was especially good at succeeding because it seemed to her she had something that other people didn't have: the desire to be alone. She had heard that the Big Apple could be a lonely place, despite the fact that you walked by hundreds of people a day. This suited Anise fine. She wanted to be invisible. She wanted to be invincible. She figured one led to the other. No one was going to use her again. No one was going to lie to her either, putting on a saint show. And no one was going to ignore her, leaving her to fend for herself. And if anyone was going to disappear, it was going to be her.

She thought these things as she left the institute, as she started her drive to Hoboken in her '77 Plymouth Volaré that she bought for $500 during her last semester. She had her map on her lap and boxes in the back. Her hair blew in the breeze. She realized she was smiling; she felt good and strong and free for a long stretch. But after an hour and a half, as the traffic picked up, as she was in a fast wash of cars, a wash that didn't and couldn't stop, and as the number of signs increased, signs that came on too fast and too many, and as she was horrified by such words as "New Jersey Turnpike" and "Lincoln Tunnel," and as sweat tricked down her temple and torso as the humidity increased, and as she viewed the dirty highways, she thought for a few minutes that she couldn't do it after all, that she was a weakling, that if she got into an accident there'd be no one to help her, that she was just a silly young woman with no experience who didn't have the right to take up residence in a city to which she had no tie. She gripped the worn steering wheel and wished the radio worked to distract her as the wind got warmer on her face.

But then the traffic stopped. Not completely, but to a crawl, and she was thankful. She exhaled, loosened her grip on the wheel and looked around at the other drivers. *Melting Pot* entered her mind for the first time she could recall, this stupid phrase, she had always thought. But it was true. There was no one type to be seen. The diversity gave her a lift because maybe she could just be one part of all these parts, all these different people making their own lives. She could be invisible here. She could do whatever she wanted.

And she wanted to do things. Anise had a plan: to crawl up the baking ladder so that eventually she could bake in a beautiful shop and go home to a beautiful apartment. She'd live a quiet life. She'd work hard making delicious food—works of art, in some cases—that people would drool over. In her quiet time at home, she'd pick up a newspaper to see what was going on in the world at large. She'd visit her dad every so often, though she didn't really want to. She'd make delicious dinners for herself. That was enough. The thought of including anyone else in that scenario exhausted her. Boyfriends and friends would disappoint or disappear. They'd leave their seed dripping down your leg or they'd stop talking to you and make other friends, even though they were your best and only friend in the world. Why put energy into that?

At the Weehawken/Hoboken exit, Anise hiccupped. She was *really* doing this, going into foreign territory, trying to live.

She entered the city, flat and industrial. It was familiar. The heat, the gray buildings. The worn buildings. The blue sky blessing its integrity. It was like Buffalo—denser and grittier, but it had to have somewhat of a similar history, Anise thought, as she drove down JFK Boulevard, a history that lay its claim in broken asphalt, in fast-food bags caught in dark corners made of concrete and steel. She knew that history. She could work with that.

She made a left on 14th street and a right onto Washington Street. This was the main drag, she could see, and her heart lifted because though it wasn't Elmwood Avenue, her favorite street in the world that she knew, it was similar. It had potential. It had shops. It had character. It had people going about their business. She liked that—people from a distance.

She reached 6th Street quickly and right away there was Bloomfield Street where she made another right. She found a parking space immediately, which would never happen again. She walked up the short flight of stairs of a rundown townhome and opened the door. Inside the hall, she rang a buzzer for apartment #1. The first door on her right opened.

"Anise or Carla? You look more like an Anise." A twenty-something girl with glossy black hair cut straight at her chin opened the door wide. She placed her hand on a hip wrapped in a black miniskirt stamped with white skulls. She looked Anise up and down and seemed to not disapprove of her old, faded t-shirt, black leggings, Birkenstocks and mass of naturally-colored, frizzy blonde curls.

"You're right." Anise was a little afraid of her. An image flashed briefly in her mind: an open mouth, bloody fangs.

"Well, c'mon in." She smiled a wide and perfect smile with white, square teeth surrounded by heavy, red lipstick. She stepped aside for Anise to enter.

"Wow, you've got a lot of stuff." Anise scanned the room.

"Ha! Did you hear that Billy? Anise says we've got a lot of stuff."

Anise turned her gaze and realized that Billy was lying on the couch. She looked around the room to see if there were others.

"It's not really all that much, love. We've gotten rid of lots. These are just the bare necessities." With that, she tossed her head back, barked one laugh, and pulled a lone cigarette out of her black tank-top.

Anise looked at the necessities, which included a white, plastic hand chair, a Native American statue with a feathered headdress, and music equipment—amps, guitars, microphone stands.

"So, Anise—God, I love that name—is that your real name?"

"Yes, my father—"

For the brief second Anise was allowed to speak, the

young woman stared at her intensely.

"Perfect. I love it! A chef who is named Anise! Isn't that great Billy?" She still hadn't lit her cigarette.

Billy lay there, blinked, and opened his mouth, having moved the pillow from off his face.

"Oh, how stupid of me. I'm Zonnie." She extended a limp and white hand.

"Is that a nickname?" Anise asked, barely touching Zonnie's hand before Zonnie took it back to wave it around while she spoke.

"You might say that." Zonnie grabbed a lighter from the top of an amp, lit her cigarette and took a drag. "Well, let me show you around." Her scuffed, black riding boots smacked on the hardwood as she sashayed toward the hallway. It turned out that Anise would be the fifth tenant of a two-bedroom apartment. The apartment had been cut up and was originally part of a family home. The two floors above made two more apartments. "So, as you know, everyone is just dying to nab a spot in Hoboken. We are, as they say, in demand." She drew out the last word. "That's why I had my friend Dino ask his friend at your Alma Mater to hang a flyer. If I were to place an ad in the paper, there would have been a deluge of lusting flat hunters. And you have to watch who you're sharing space with. There are some fucking weirdos out there!"

Zonnie talked as she opened the bathroom door, as she walked down the narrow hallway, as she showed Anise the bedroom she shared with Billy. "Kurt is spoiled. He gets the best room. Asthma. He hides in there with the ceiling fan while he smokes one fag after another. He's in there now. 'Kurt, are you decent or do you have your bloody wanker flopping in the breeze?'" Zonnie chuckled at her own joke, snorting into her hand, endearing Anise to her in that gesture. "Ugh. He's probably dead. You can view his corpse later."

They walked back down the hall.

"Are you British? Anise asked.

Zonnie stopped in her tracks and whipped around, giving Anise the stare.

"It's just that, your words, and I thought I detected an—"

Zonnie sighed and leaned back against the stucco with her eyes closed. "Don't I wish." After three seconds of silence, her eyes opened wide. "Do you know that Sid Vicious's mother killed him?" Zonnie locked a fierce glower on Anise. "She gave him heroin, and he dropped dead—his own fucking mother!" Zonnie released her gaze. "Okay. Let's take a look-see at your digs."

They walked to the living room, the only other room besides the small kitchen, which Anise glanced at and thought she caught sight of a cat perched on an overflowing counter, licking inside a pot.

"Billy, get up. Give Anise her bed."

"My bed?"

"Don't look so horrified, love. You've got the best room in the house. It's the biggest."

"But, what about privacy?" Anise saw no way this could be possible.

"You should see what they're doing upstairs! One guy has a free-standing pisser in his bedroom." Zonnie took a drag and blew it to the ceiling.

"It's just—I'm a private person." Anise crossed her arms, hugged herself. She had always thought she was open-minded, on the edge of society even, but now she felt like a prudish old woman from what she imagined Connecticut looked like. Buttoned up. Lace colors. A cardigan. "Wait. You said I was the fifth tenant. Who is the other?"

Billy kicked a lump on the other end of the couch. Anise had thought it was just a blanket.

"What the fuck." A muscular guy emerged.

"Meet Matt. Our drummer." Zonnie said and knocked on her head with her knuckles as she widened her eyes at Anise.

"Hey," he greeted and then pulled the blanket back over him.

Zonnie shook her head like a mother who was at her wits end. "Anyway, that's Matt. He sort of sleeps wherever. Since he gives the smallest amount of rent, he really doesn't have say. So, he'll probably be in the hallway most of the time. Yes, that will work." Zonnie nodded, calculating all the variables.

Anise was actually relieved to hear that, and somehow, with that information, her perspective changed, and the living room didn't seem so bad. "Do you mind if I change things around?"

Zonnie shook her head with an expression that announced she didn't understand why anyone would want to do such a thing. "No, no. Go right ahead."

Anise smiled her crooked smile, causing Zonnie to brighten, lift her shoulders in delight, and smile back.

****

By the end of the day, Anise had brought her stuff in from the car and rearranged the living room. She turned the sofa around so that it faced the wall, shoving it in the corner. She figured if she didn't do that, she'd find Matt passed out in it. She wanted something tall for privacy, like a dressing screen. There was the Indian and a microphone stand and one of her sheets. This would do for now. She didn't ask; she just used them. Desperate times, as they say. Everything else she made as nice as she could, the white hand chair facing the window, amps under the sill, a broken coffee table in-between. She stacked CDs and old records neatly on the floor against one wall. On a box of something heavy, she spread her blue pillowcase. On top of that, she placed an unremarkable lamp that shone bright glare, causing Anise to wince. Anise looked around, noticed a piece of red, torn material, hugging a dusty corner. Anise shook it, coughed, and hung it over the lamp shade.

"There," she said, always happy to reveal what might otherwise be hidden forever.

Zonnie, Billy and Matt had gone out for breakfast, even though they left at 4:00 PM and now it was 6:00 P.M. Kurt hadn't surfaced. Anise had forgotten about him until she heard something drop, which made her jump and touch her chest. She thought she heard another noise, and feeling like a character in a horror movie who walks toward impending doom, Anise made her way down the hall quietly. Once at Kurt's door, she put her ear against it, thinking she could hear the soft thud of a spinning fan. Out of the corner of her eye, she detected movement in the galley kitchen, directly across Kurt's room. She turned her head.

"Ahh!" Anise let out a high yell and tensed up as she watched the gray cat from earlier jump to the floor and run past her, into the living room. Still, no movement from Kurt. She gathered her wits and walked into the kitchen. "Oh. My. God." Anise was always up for a challenge, but there were greasy stripes on the wall above the stove. There was cereal with mold in the sink. There was cat food and hairy water on the floor in the corner with what she guessed was a hairball nearby. In her belongings in the living room, still unpacked, were cooking utensils, and as she looked around, she couldn't imagine adding them to this mess. She was tired, overwhelmed. She hugged herself, yet again. "It's just temporary. That's all. Just until I find something better. Make more money." She opened the cupboard door under the sink to see a mouse caught in a trap. "Oh, god. Oh, god." She slammed the cupboard door and brought her hand to her mouth.

The apartment door opened and Zonnie's exclamations could be heard over the others as they viewed the organization, the finesse. Anise wiped her teary eyes as she heard Zonnie's boots smacking wood.

"Anise, the room looks fab!" Zonnie squealed and

quick-stepped to Anise while holding groceries, then landed an air-kiss on her cheek. "I have something for you." Zonnie looked for a place to set her bag and realized there was no counter space, so she reached into the bag, pulled out the item that was inside and tossed the bag to the floor. She held a head-sized object wrapped in white butcher paper. "Guess what this is."

Anise had an idea, but she didn't want to burst Zonnie's bubble by guessing correctly.

"Cucumbers?" Anise lied.

"No, silly." Zonnie tore open the paper and grabbed the two wings of a headless, fresh chicken and made it dance in the air like a puppet. "It's a chicken. You can cook it tonight for dinner. We haven't had a home-cooked meal in ages and seeing that we have a real, live, professional cook in the house, we thought it was time. We paid for it; you cook it. Deal?"

"Tonight?" Anise asked, looking around the kitchen.

"Oh, I guess you're right. It *is* a little messy. Okay then. Tomorrow." She wrapped up the chicken so that most was exposed and crammed it in the small refrigerator, closing the door quickly. "We ate already anyway. Going to lie down for a while, love. We've got a show tonight, and I need my beauty sleep. Ta-ta!" She headed for her bedroom and Billy followed.

"So, what exactly do you play?" Anise asked, causing them both to turn around and stare. Zonnie spoke.

"Mostly originals, with a few covers."

"Cool. What do you sound like?"

Zonnie opened her mouth to speak but Billy spoke first, startling Anise because she figured he gave up when he met Zonnie.

"You know Simple Minds?" He leaned against the door frame, his leather jacket making him look confident and tough.

"Sure." Anise didn't like the band but didn't let on.

"Bon Jovi?"

It seemed an odd combination, and Anise was both disappointed and surprised, but she remained courteous.

"Uh-huh."

"Bruce Springsteen?"

"Yeah, but—"

"We don't sound like any of that shit."

Zonnie snorted. Billy smiled, crossed his arms.

Anise smiled then stopped abruptly, realizing she was the joke. They assumed she knew nothing about music because she didn't wear it on her sleeve like Billy did with his band stickers on his leather jacket, something she might have done in high school with her teased bangs and army jacket, when she scratched The Misfits in pen on her bookbag.

At that moment, she felt much older than her roommates, seasoned, a woman with an education who knew how to clean a kitchen, who didn't size people up or play stupid games.

"I would *hope* you don't sound like that shit." Anise walked toward them, so they had to split up in the tiny space and part for her to get by. She turned around once she was in the hall. "I pegged you more for X or maybe The Germs." She made her way to the living room, biting her lip while smiling, the image of their dropped jaws fresh in her mind.

Zonnie and Billy closed their bedroom behind them. All was quiet. Anise crawled over the arm of the sofa and lay down, realizing Matt was not in the house. She wondered where he was, where his stuff was, if he had any belongings at all. She pulled a blanket up to her chin. It was a hot, summer evening, but she wanted something to cover her.

This wouldn't be so bad. It was a start. She couldn't afford being on her own, but she could see it in her mind, just out of reach but not unreachable: a lovely little place. A clean place with windows and sun. A place to retreat to after unleashing little, delicious masterpieces that waited to be born. Inside bags of flour, inside skins of lemons, inside shells of eggs.

Anise woke the next morning, at four, as the band came in the house. Each one grunted as they entered the apartment, dragging amps, guitars and now Matt's drum kit in pieces that must have had a temporary home elsewhere. No one spoke, and Anise couldn't see them from her side of the curtain. As quickly as they appeared, they vanished behind doors, all but Matt of whom Anise caught sight, pulling a green sleeping bag and a pillow from a pile of clothes. It was the one area of the living room Anise hadn't dared to touch when she saw underwear in the pile. As he lay in the hall, she thought that certainly there'd be room for him in this fairly large room if only they'd organize. She shook her head in the dark, realizing she was meddling into people's lives, and really, did she want Matt sleeping just yards away?

She was wide awake, and since she had an appointment at noon in Manhattan, she decided to get up and take a shower while it was available, as well as consult her bus and train maps, having been warned earlier by Zonnie that driving in the city was impossible and there'd be no place to park. She peeled down her blanket, opened her suitcase that contained all her clothes, pulled out khakis, a capped-sleeve blouse, and a lightweight, wrinkle-free blazer with shoulder pads that she shook out and lay over the edge of the couch. She grabbed toiletries and a towel and headed toward the shower, walking over snoring Matt.

****

What a lift of confidence! Forty minutes from her door in Hoboken, New Jersey to Christopher Street in the West Village of Manhattan. The bus, easy. The Path train, easy. A lot of people, but a straightforward trip, and the best part was that it was true: She could disappear. No one cared. No one smiled, but you couldn't smile at a person you passed because then you'd have a constant grin stuck to your face. There were just too many people for that. No, just go where you need to go.

The architecture! Even trees on Christopher Street. Old buildings tucked one against another, no space wasted. Potential being used. She got it. She understood the appeal. Elmwood, her lovely Elmwood Avenue back in Buffalo, now seemed a sad little strip in comparison.

Bleeker Street had more grit, more of a get-down-to-business feel, less of a stroll, more paper in the gutter, no trees, and an interview for a bakery chef assistant.

Anise opened the door of Gino's and knew she had to be there, knew she had to get the job. Not only was she greeted with glorious air conditioning, but her eyes beheld the longest glass case of Italian pastries she had ever seen. And beyond the case were many tables, and beyond that, a courtyard. An urban paradise.

A line had formed, and Anise pondered the best way to navigate this situation. How would a New Yorker do it? Would she interrupt the service, state she was here for an interview, or get in line? She decided to do both. She got in line and as soon as she caught the eye of a dark-haired man behind the counter, she said, "Excuse me."

He didn't respond with words, but offered eye-contact: *Make it quick. We're busy here.*

"I'm here for the interview?"

"Oh, yeah. Go to the back, second door past the restroom."

"Great, thanks." On the way to the back, Anise saw these:

> Lobster tails (flaky pastry with cream filling)
> Pasticiotti (flaky pastry with cream filling)
> Sfogliatella (flaky pastry with cream filling)
> Cannoli (flaky pastry with cream filling)

And many other delights that were made with other

things besides cream filling. But Anise understood that most pastry should, indeed, have cream filling. She understood this well. She wondered if they made pasticiotti with almond paste, too. Almond paste was the only filling that rivaled a creamy one, and a ricotta-based creamy filling was the only cream that could hold its own against almond paste.

At the appropriate door, Anise knocked, another gesture that she wasn't sure a New Yorker would do. No one answered, so she knocked harder. The same man who had been at the counter opened it.

"Oh. How did you do that?" In her surprise, she forgot about formality and New York indifference. He responded with a smile, which took her aback. Maybe when there was a reason to communicate in New York, things slowed down enough for any expression at all.

"Come into my office."

His office was a metal desk in a small, unattractive room with metal file cabinets and bright lights. He sat down, his white apron covering his knees and seeming to be part of his very person. He had a pencil behind his ear, like a man from another era, but he seemed youngish, not an old guy, maybe forty.

"Gino." He put out his hand.

"You're Gino?" She put out her hand, but was too distracted with the information to be assertive.

He smiled. "The second. I took over the business."

"Oh, I see." She nodded.

"So," He held her faxed résumé in a tight grip. She had painstakingly composed it on an electric typewriter at the institute. "This is a first for us."

"First?" She thought he meant interviewing someone with no real job experience. It was true. Her only paid experience was working at a drug store and an ice-cream shop during the summers, which got her through the school year and for this first month of rent, gas, toothpaste. She needed more money and paid work experience, that was clear.

"First time hiring outside of the family."

"Oh?" She was relieved but didn't let on.

"Yeah, well. You put your whole life into something, bring up your kids the way you were brought up—hard work, family, tradition, respect, loyalty—and they go and decide they don't want any of it."

Anise couldn't imagine having a father care so much about holding everyone's lives all together like that, being so present, involved.

"Sorry about that. You don't need to hear that. It's not your concern."

"Personally, I can't imagine not wanting to work here. I honestly don't know what would be better."

He took in a deep breath and exhaled. "You're hired."

"What? You haven't even asked me questions."

"I don't have to. You have a degree. You have raving recommendations from your instructors. It's clear you know how to make pastry—am I right?"

"Yes, you're right." Anise sat with a straight back. Her fingers were laced.

"But most importantly, you got something else. Do you know what that is?" He leaned into his hand on his apron-covered leg.

"Potential?"

"No. Desire. Your cover letter says it all. You've been cooking since you were a kid. You cooked for your family."

Anise bit her lip. It was the first time she heard that from someone else's mouth.

"You okay with the hours? Sometimes it is overnight."

"I'm a night owl. I like peace and quiet, when everyone else is sleeping." She said it dreamily, with confidence, sure he would agree.

"Well, good luck with that! It's pretty noisy here at night."

Her face heated up with embarrassment. "Of course.

That makes sense." She continued to take a stab at maturity. "I'll save that for my retirement, then."

Gino nodded. "Well, before you sign your life away, let me tell you more. I can only pay you a little bit more than minimum wage—I got to do the figures. It's a lot of work. You may get a break—you may not. It depends on who's working. I need someone full-time, that means every day—or night, depending. We try to mix it up so that everyone gets a good night sleep once in a while, though it doesn't really happen because your body aint used to it. Still, people are needed here 'round the clock because we're open from morning until midnight, and we always have customers—that's another thing. You'll have to serve customers. Everyone here pitches in with everything. No one's a prima donna or a prince. I design wedding cakes and I clean toilets. I won't ask you to clean toilets—yet. Still interested?"

"We learned about hours and hard work in school. I'm ready to do it."

"Learning is one thing. Doing is another."

Anise, always a quick-learner, realized she needed to speak his language.

"Give me a chance. Let me prove it to you. I didn't go to cooking school to think about it; I went to do it."

Gino smiled. "Come with me. I'll show you around."

****

Anise couldn't remember being this happy. As she walked up the stairs from the Path train in Hoboken, she held her blazer over her arm and her step was light. She wanted to share her success. She wanted to call her dad, but she didn't have a phone. The apartment didn't have a phone. She could gather quarters and call from a phone booth, but she needed her money. She didn't want to call collect because who knew how much that would cost and this wasn't an emergency.

As she walked up Bloomfield, she looked at the cars on the street, knowing hers was just ahead. She felt the weight of the car, of figuring out how she was going to move it to the opposite side of the street when required, of paying for insurance and gas. Standing in front of her apartment, she still saw no car. Stolen. There was no other possibility. She had parked correctly. "Well, okay, then," she said, scanning the street. "That takes care of that." Anise headed up the steps (At the police station later that week, she would fill out paperwork and as she would walk away from the cop chewing gum, she would catch his smirk as he tossed her form in a high stack).

Opening the door to her apartment, she jumped because there was a young man sitting in the white hand, facing the window. He turned.

"Hey," he said.

"Hey?"

"You must be Anise." He got out of the hand and put out his, looking at her directly with blue eyes. Shadows underneath only intensified the blue. "Kurt."

She exhaled. "Oh, now I get it. Nice to meet you." And it was. A serene presence in the apartment was refreshing. She found herself curious. After her great morning with Gino, she was in touch with her outgoing side.

"So, Kurt. What brings you to Hoboken? And how did you join the band?" She kicked off her shoes, laid her blazer over the couch. "Is there any coffee in that scary kitchen?"

"God, there better be. I just bought some yesterday. Let's look." Kurt stood again and walked past Anise. His dirty blonde, straight hair actually was dirty, but somehow, it worked. His feet were bare. He wore baggy shorts. He didn't quite fit with the others—then again, neither did Matt the drummer, but Matt seemed disposable.

"Where are you from, originally?" She followed him into the kitchen, feeling like an older woman in a business suit compared to his laid-back stride and clothes. She wished she had on her leggings and t-shirt.

"Originally?" he said, as he opened a cupboard above the sink. "L.A."

"Ohhh," Anise responded knowingly, though she knew nothing about Los Angeles.

"Been there?" He looked at her, then at the cupboard, reaching for a pound of coffee, smelling in the bag.

She hadn't seen anyone smell food like that outside of her fellow students and instructors. It distracted her. "No, no. You just don't seem…east coast."

"*That* I'm not." He filled a teakettle and turned on the stove. He then rinsed a stained carafe that was underneath a Styrofoam takeout container and placed a Melitta cone on top and a filter inside. Anise liked that he knew the process.

"What don't you like about this area? Besides the dirt, mice, people." Anise crossed her arms, leaned on the doorframe.

"I guess it's the dirt, mice, people." He smiled. "No, not really. I mean," and he yawned and stretched his arms above his head so his taut stomach peeked out, "we have that in L.A., for sure. But I'm more about the beach. And treating my body well. You don't really have that around here."

"I hear the New Jersey beaches are nice."

"Yeahhh. It's fine, it's fine." He looked around the kitchen, as if he couldn't find what he needed.

"So, how do you pay the rent?" Anise asked.

"I'm living off an inheritance. This is considered college funding. I'm taking a semester off."

She nodded while she thought, *Lazy*.

He smiled a little smile. Made no attempt to find out about her life, past, interests. Anise smiled a little smile and left the kitchen, brought her old shorts and t-shirt into the bathroom to change, gearing up to clean the kitchen. As she changed, she mentally bookmarked how it is good to ask questions, how quickly you can get the facts, how a clearer perspective on an individual, for instance, can be achieved in minutes. How cream can sour overnight. How time doesn't have to be wasted getting to know the wrong people.

Kurt walked into his bedroom with a steamy cup while Anise opened the bathroom door. "Coffee's ready." He said.

"Great. Thanks."

He blew in his cup, shut the door behind him.

Anise brought her clothes back to her suitcase.

Zonnie came in the apartment. "Hi, love! How did it go?"

Funny how someone who before seemed fake seemed real in comparison.

"Thanks for asking, Zonnie." Anise put her fists up in the air. "I got the job!"

"Hurray, hurrah! Congratulations! Now we won't be kicked out. Let's celebrate. What should we do? Should we go down to Maxwell's tonight? Or maybe someplace else. We just played there last night. I get bored easily."

"Hold on, Zonnie. I appreciate your enthusiasm. But no. I have a job and it starts tomorrow. I won't be going out much—if ever. I'll be baking at all hours, often overnight."

"That blows." Zonnie sunk to the floor and crisscrossed her legs. This day she wore torn jeans and a billowy white shirt.

"I don't think it blows. I'm happy. This is my first real job. And it's why I went to school. I'm ecstatic!" Anise walked to the kitchen, still wanting that coffee.

"Well, when you put it that way, I'm jealous." She hollered from the living room.

"It's just something I've always wanted—do you want coffee?" Anise hollered back.

"Yeah, sure," Zonnie's voice trailed off.

When Anise returned with two cups of black coffee

since there was no milk in the fridge or sugar to be found, she found Zonnie lying on her back on the floor, knees up, staring at the ceiling.

"What's the matter?"

"I don't know what I want." A tear rolled down her temple.

"Well, you're in a band. That's a very cool thing. Aren't you happy in it? Do you guys have a plan to make a record deal?" Anise sat cross-legged on the floor.

Zonnie's voice got louder, and she drew out her words. "Oh, yeah, sure, we've got plans." She covered her eyes with the back of her hand. "Just like every other band." She sat up and grabbed her cigarettes from a little red purse. "But I want more. And if I can't go to the top, then I want out." She lit her cigarette with a slim Zippo.

Anise wanted a cigarette right then only because of the snap of the lighter when Zonnie closed the lid. She hadn't thought about smoking for a while. She fought the urge. Tomorrow was her new job. She didn't want to reek.

"Why can't you get to the top?" Anise sipped her coffee.

"Because odds are against us. And no one else wants it. Billy is happy playing bass even in the smallest venues, even once a month. Matt's only been with us for a month and Kurt is an amazing guitar player and songwriter, but he'll get his degree or surf or whatever. And I can tell that he's going to ditch us. It's been me and Billy the longest." Zonnie's shoulders were hanging.

"What does making it to the top mean, anyway?" Anise stretched out on her side, head in her hand. "Unless you're playing Top-Forty, how can you make it to the top?"

"The top of punk, Anise. It's not very high. But it was a goal." She took a drag, blew it out. Zonnie looked older, beaten down.

"What about doing music and something else, too? What are your other interests? How do you pay the rent?"

"I'm a fucking nanny, Anise!"

"A nanny?"

"Yes." Her voice softened to a whisper. "And I love it. I love babies." She said this with droopy, apologetic eyes."

"Really?"

"Oh, Anise. They are so innocent, so sweet. They will never hurt you like everyone else in this world. They just want to be cared for."

Anise couldn't recall seeing a baby up close.

"The parents don't mind that you look like that? I mean—" Anise pictured babies covered in red kisses with cigarette smoke wafting all around.

"They don't see me like this. I go three days a week and tone it way down, believe me."

"I think that you should—"

"How did you know you wanted to cook?" Zonnie's eyes beckoned.

"It's a long story, Zonnie. I don't think you want to hear it." Anise rubbed the rim of her cup with her thumb.

"Like hell I don't." She put out her cigarette. "I demand you tell me every disgusting detail about sausage or pies or whatever the hell got you into this."

Anise exhaled. "Okay. Well. It started with a cookbook—no. It started way before that. It started, it started when my mother died. Could I have one of those cigarettes?" Anise pleaded.

****

One month had passed. Anise was coming into her own. Gino approved of her work. She waited on customers happily—more happily then necessary—since she wasn't a native New Yorker and didn't mind having a semi-permanent grin stuck to her face, especially because it was real. She baked cheesecakes one after another as if she'd done it for years. Gino was even considering letting her add almond pasticiotti to the menu, at least on a trial basis. She got along with his two daughters who were still committed to the business (she hadn't seen his son, the traitor). On day twenty-five, Gino's mother asked for her help with ricotta filling, to which Anise took to heart as if it was a dubbing of knighthood. The daughters noticed and smiled as they rolled dough. Anise was in.

She walked up the steps of the train station and felt at home in Hoboken. As had been the case these quick weeks, Anise walked to her apartment in anticipation of talking with Zonnie, of sharing the funny things of the day, the challenges, the successes. She had cried the day she shared her story with Zonnie, who had petted her head, had shushed her, had shooed Billy and Matt away. Anise had learned of Zonnie's childhood, of the abuse she had endured, of why, it was clear to Anise, she was so conflicted, why she wanted to both cuddle babies and scream "fuck you" into a microphone.

Anise ran up the steps, opened the front door and fiddled with her key since the apartment door was locked. Inside, the room was almost empty. No hand chair, no amps, no microphone stands. Matt's pile was gone. Anise dropped her purse and marched to the door at the end of the hall, and as she got closer, her stomach began to sink because she could see the door was ajar, and it never was ajar. She pushed it open. Empty, except for dust and a hanger in the closet.

At Kurt's door, she stopped. She could hear the spinning of the fan. She knocked, but he didn't answer, so she tried the knob, and it was locked. She felt some relief because it wasn't total abandonment. Not to mention that Kurt paid a good portion of the rent.

She stopped at the kitchen, the kitchen she scrubbed clean, the kitchen that Zonnie helped to paint, the kitchen they laughed in. Her eyes darted around, searching for a note. She opened the fridge—that would be something Zonnie would do, something out of the ordinary, something fun, something that would show she was thinking of Anise. Nothing. She zoomed into the living room, scanned her things. Nothing there either. She looked at the windows, at the breezy curtains and sun coming through. She held back tears. She looked at the lone Indian. A cigar store Indian, an antique maybe. A nasty thing. It spoke of things that weren't true. It spoke of lies. It spoke of taking what isn't yours and leaving you in the dust.

Anise dragged the heavy thing across the floor, scratching wood against wood, history gouging history. She opened the door, pulled it into the hallway of the building, grunting. Once over the threshold and on the landing, she shoved the Indian, watched its head hit the pavement, watched it roll onto the sidewalk. She slammed the door of the building, went inside.

In the apartment, Anise grabbed her notepad, the thing she used to plan her life. She tore the last two pages from it, balled them up tight, threw them to the floor. From a habit she adopted during the month, she began to sit at a certain spot on the floor, but she stopped midway down and bolted up. There would be none of that. There would be none of anything that reminded her of sharing with Zonnie.

She put her notepad on the sofa, about to hop over, then stopped and pulled the sofa around. She sat down and began her list. Her new plan was titled, "Anise's Life," underlined with three dark lines. The first three things on the list were:

1. Move into bedroom
2. Discuss rent with Kurt
3. Don't let people fuck with you

Up the Ladder

Anise applied point number three of her list at work, too. After Zonnie and her boys departed, Anise arrived the next day courteous and pleasant, but there was no smile stuck to her face. There was no asking questions to the sisters about growing up in the city. She rolled pastry. She mixed filling. She leveled flour. She offered small, polite smiles. Whether or not Gino's mother asked for butter was of no concern to Anise. Anise was not part of their family and never would be.

Six months had passed since Anise moved into Zonnie and Billy's room. Kurt paid half the rent during that time, six hundred dollars. The day he left he didn't give notice either but was just gone one day, which felt natural. Anise didn't go to her landlord to inform him she needed another roommate (she had never met him, anyway); instead, she taped one little ad in the window at Gino's and received twenty phone calls (she had gotten a phone the month before) in one hour on one Saturday afternoon. She was explicit in what she wanted: a quiet female with a steady job (and no personality that she could detect. If the female sounded at all bubbly or adventurous, she crossed her name off the list as she spoke). Call twenty-one was the lucky winner: Doris, a forty-nine-year-old divorcee who worked as a receptionist at St. Vincent's Hospital. She mentioned that she liked to crochet in her room with her small TV. *No need for an interview. Just bring your stuff over next week.*

For six months, Doris was a perfect roommate, and Anise was, too. They both took care of their own things, and little things that would normally bug roommates didn't because they didn't get close emotionally, so they didn't get on each other's nerves. Instead, they engaged in brief small-talk if they should pass. They didn't offer each other their leftovers or share milk or toothpaste. They cleaned their own hair out of the drain after showering. Neither entertained. They had both been hurt, and they both knew relationships of any kind would simply lead to pain. Plus, Anise was often sleeping in the evenings, so they hardly ever saw each other.

It had been a year since Anise had been working at Gino's, and she realized she had gone as far as she could go. She wasn't family, so she wouldn't manage or inherit the shop. Gino's mother would not allow a change to the menu because her husband put it together and *God rest his soul* (the rest of the words were spoken in loud Italian to Gino who yelled back). Gino had stepped into the front of the shop where Anise was handing biscotti to a customer. He wiped his hands on his apron and simply said, "No almond pasticiotti" and walked away. She watched him depart and knew it was time.

After work, which ended on this day at 4:30 P.M., she read *The New York Times* classifieds on her walk to the Path train and stopped in her tracks when she saw an ad for an assistant pastry chef at a big hotel in the heart of Manhattan near Grand Central Station. Her heart picked up speed. It was time to step out of her comfort zone. She needed a challenge. She needed more money. As it was, she was using all her money to pay the rent, pay a modest student loan payment, get to work, wash her clothes and eat.

The ad gave an address to send the résumé. Anise realized copies of her résumé at the apartment were missing her job experience.

"Excuse me," Anise spoke to a dog-walker who was harnessing three small pure-breds.

"Can you tell me where the library is?"

"On the corner of 10th and 6th Avenue," he said without stopping his herd.

"Thanks!" Anise headed in that direction. It wasn't far at all. As she walked, she hoped they would let her type a letter, even if she didn't have a library card. It was at times like this that she realized she needed to be a little more attached to the world at large, the bigger community—especially if she was going to work at a big hotel. She had to interact more. She would have to force herself to.

She turned her gaze upward off the pavement, shook out her hair that had been tied back in a ponytail, took a deep breath. She would be okay. All these people in New York, she told herself, didn't care about her, remember? That's what she told herself when she arrived. She could blend in and disappear. She just had to be careful, keep her distance, do what Gino's mom did, keep it within the family—even if she was a family of one.

She pursed her lips, walked fast. When a young couple sauntered by, hand-in-hand on this sunny, late afternoon, smiling and laughing, Anise's cold eyes glazed over and past them. Obviously, they were tourists and didn't know any better.

****

On Anise's last day of work, she fought feeling sheepish. She knew they gave her a chance, opened up their home business, showed her how they did things, things that had been done for three generations—and now she was leaving. She knew that she turned on them another way, too. She turned inward; she put on her emotional armor; she snuffed her light before one of them would.

But at this moment, she was the only one waiting on customers, and she was getting irritated. Four other people were on the premises, and they left her alone— which was against the rule; there was supposed to be two up front, at least, one to serve and one to ring up orders— and the customers were getting antsy, and three more just walked in.

"Excuse me," she said. Anise shook her head and wiped her hands on her apron while she walked fast to the kitchen and pushed the door open.

"Surprise!" Gino and family hollered.

"What?" Anise said.

"What, she says. What d'ya mean, what?" Gino said as he walked toward her. A white cake with Star Anise decorations stood tall on the table. "Congratulations." He grasped her arms with his dry, tired hands. "We're happy for you. You've got to move on to bigger things. That's why you went to school."

"But I—" Anise covered her mouth. Tears filled her eyes, and everyone was blurry, but she didn't want them to be blurry because this was it, and she couldn't see his mother's expression, and she thought that maybe she was crying, too, but then she shook her silly thought away and looked down and before she knew it, Gino's mom was in front of her.

"You show them how to do it, Anise. You show them all, eh? You come back and tell us how it goes, eh? Okay. Okay, now."

Off the Ladder

Anise walked through the hotel pastry kitchen, checking on progress and order. The kitchen was Anise's home, since most of her time was spent there, in a sea of aluminum and confections and white uniforms. She had worked hard these last nine years at the hotel and was now the Assistant Executive Pastry Chef. She had a good team, and she worked under the Executive Pastry Chef, Joe, her mentor, whose fits of rage got things done. He had screamed at her through the first year and then just stopped. This seemed to be the way. Anise watched the pattern with new staff through the years. She saw that it took a good year for new cooks to get it all. You either sank or swam, and if you swam, you swam stronger in the end because you had gone to your limits—emotional and physical—and returned.   Anise had witnessed that everyone who made it through this culinary correctional program was tougher. Thick-skinned souls would then bloom gelatin in water, spread mousse with the lightest touch onto thin feuilletine. They'd carefully plate their delicate desserts, then they'd send them off, never to witness the closing of dreamy eyes when a bite was taken.

Since the end of Anise's first year at the hotel, she felt at ease. After all, she'd been in the kitchen since she was a kid. And as much as she depended on no one in her private life, she understood that every baker in the kitchen was only one part of a bigger whole. And as much as cooks thought of their coworkers as family, Anise did not. And no matter how calm she was when in charge, she remained humorless. She didn't punch the cutting board like Joe when things were slipping; she simply frowned and remained silent, which worked just as well. She knew how to praise, too. When Anise said, "This is good," the pastry chef or assistant pastry chef or student would know that they had made something very, very good.

If eager staff had ideas on how to improve a technique or recipe, they would go to Anise before Joe because a quiet, reasoned denial was easier on the ego than a loud and final, "No." Anise still had a memory of such a time that stung from her first year. She had gone to Joe with her almond pasticiotti idea that still lingered from the year before, at Gino's.

"Pasticiotti? Pasticiotti is everywhere in New York," Joe scoffed. "It isn't special, memorable. It will do nothing for the restaurant, for the hotel." Joe counted bags of flour. "Think of the big picture, Anise, not just your little desires."

She had felt her face heat up as his voice boomed through the kitchen, as she walked back to her station, looking at the floor. But she was a trooper and had come back the next day.

"I've got another idea." Anise stood at attention with her hands clasped, her apron clean, her blonde wispy curls neat in her ponytail. "I'm thinking of using an almond filling but in a cannoli shell instead of a tart, only napoleon style." She looked for a twinkle in his eye at the last part, the twist, the thing that made it special: napoleon style cannoli with almond filling. You didn't get *that* in every bakery. "I'm still playing with it."

Joe stopped rotating items in the refrigerator. "And what are you planning on doing with this idea?"

Immediately, Anise realized her boldness and felt her face heat up again. "I, uh, I guess, I'm just experimenting." She hurried back to her spot.

The rest of that day, Anise doubted her ability, and it stayed with her through the years. She still rose to countless challenges, but one thing she didn't do was take risks. She observed, learned and worked hard, but she played it safe. And you can't become an outstanding pastry chef if you play it safe year after year.

If Anise would have shared her emotions with others in the kitchen, she would have blossomed, would have dazzled the eye and the stomach. But she kept her pains to herself, so she didn't get to hear the other assistants say *He can fuck himself!* She didn't get to huddle and gossip and grow strong in the words of a friend who understands, who says, *I know!* In this one area, Anise sunk.

These days, Anise was generally content because she was proud of her work. But Anise churned out the same five menu items again and again and spent more than half her time managing the kitchen. The quiet joy of creating was gone. Joe was tapping into it lately, experimenting in his own little world with flowers and ganache, rhubarb and meringue, yelling at his ingredients.

On this day, he had handed the kitchen over completely to Anise for two hours, and he was not to be bothered. His signature dish from five years ago was still on the menu—Raspberry & Lemon Mousse Cake w/Chocolate Pistachios. Individual-sized molds were used, and the customers were always happy. Anise understood though. A chef gets antsy. A customer gets bored. A restaurant gets stagnant. New, delicious items on a fresh menu cause sparks, create buzz. Just as a sizzling flambé turns heads, a new to-die-for dessert gets people talking.

Anise had experienced this—the energy in the kitchen, increasing or decreasing with the simple addition of something new—a desert item, a sous chef, a remark.

Anise wanted to see what Joe was doing, so she delegated the order intake to the pastry chef who was next in charge.

"I envy you. What are you making?" Anise stood close, aware of the proximity. No matter how many years they'd work together, she still felt like a student to his mastery, never his equal.

Joe glared at her for a moment, looking both angry and bewildered, having been pulled out of deep concentration. As he began to talk, he softened.

"I've been struggling with coming up with a variation on almond pasticiotti. I—"

"Almond pasticiotti?"

"Yes," Joe said, "and I think I've got it. I haven't tried it yet, but I have the idea: cannoli napoleon with ricotta and almond mousse."

"Cannoli napoleon?" Anise asked, feeling her face go white. She held the edge of the work table.

"Yes. Can you see it? A cannoli napoleon but with alternate layers of almond mousse and ricotta filling. Cannoli is best when filled—"

"When filled to order so the shells don't get soft," Anise said, "which would work with the mousse as well since the mousse has to stay refrigerated."

"Exactly!" Joe said, grabbing her arms.

She continued. "It wouldn't be hard, since everything is made in advance. If we get an order, we simply assemble and plate."

"You've got it!" He jumped up and down.

She pulled herself out of her trance. "Tell me, Joe. What was your inspiration?"

"My grandmother." Joe looked into his memories. "She made the best cannoli I've ever tasted."

"Just your grandmother?" Anise wiped her hands on her apron, again and again.

"Yeah, why do you ask?"

She looked into his face, straight on. He really didn't know. If her suggestion years ago had sunk deep into his mind's baking files, he was clueless. So much weight she had put into his passing comment, a comment she carried with her, a comment that she let mold her, and he didn't even remember.

"No reason." Anise said. She walked away, took over the orders, the management of the kitchen. She moved through the kitchen fast, glancing at oblivious Joe. A veil had been lifted. Cold water had been splashed. Her eyes darted around. It was time to make decisions. Changes had to be made.

Anise took a seat on the Path train. She hadn't moved from her apartment in Hoboken. It wasn't worth it, to move into the city, pay twice as much for half the space. Two years ago, her roommate, Doris, moved to Florida, her ultimate dream: palm trees and sun. Anise nodded as she was jostled by the train, as she stared out the window, at the ugly wash of gray tunnel and dull tile. She thought how Doris had it right, how she had a goal and nothing was going to stop her from getting it.

Thirty minutes later, Anise stepped off the Path train and boarded the bus for the ten-minute ride home down Washington Street. Things were going to be different, this she knew, as she looked out the bus window on this dark and rainy night.

As she approached her stop, she noticed that Seventh Street was partially blocked off, so the bus was going to have to make a detour. The door opened for her and one other person, and when it did, she smelled smoke. She hurried off the bus, took a few steps onto the sidewalk and opened her umbrella, beginning the short walk down

Seventh Street to Bloomfield.

She could now see the smoke, rising from the very area she was headed. It wasn't the first time she witnessed a fire in Hoboken. Anise had seen others, too. Rumors had it they were intentional, that old apartment buildings were set ablaze expertly so that the innards would fry while the frame stood solid. The "old-timers" would have to leave—if they made it out alive—so the newcomers who worked in New York could come and pay good money for a rebuilt condo. Anise picked up her pace as she realized that though she wasn't an old-timer, her apartment was old. She didn't pay the fixed rents that the old-timers did; she paid an average sum. But the renter on the third floor, what about him? Wasn't he an old guy who had lived there for many years? She had kept to herself, had never spoken to him, never asked him if he needed help, knew nothing about him.

Anise turned the corner of her street, which was blocked off from traffic. Two fire trucks filled the narrow street, like noisy, blinking monsters. Neighbors whom Anise never spoke to stared at her building. Flames and smoke shot out of the two, top-floor windows and one of the second-floor windows. A fireman on a ladder rose high until he directed a hose toward the window. Anise watched the water blast at the flames.

Anise pushed through the crowd and ran up the short flight of stairs to the apartment building before anyone could stop her, clutching her purse, well aware that it might be all she had left. Once inside the hallway, she heard steps on the stairs and saw smoke making its way down. She unlocked her door with a shaking hand. Standing in the apartment, she looked around for what she should take. She ran to the back, to her bedroom, and started pulling clothes off hangers, holding a pile. Running to the bathroom, she grabbed her toothpaste and toothbrush. Into the kitchen, she ran, everything a blur as she scanned all her work, her clean kitchen that she hardly ever used. She smelled smoke and began to cough, dropping the things she collected as she yanked open drawers.

"Ma'am, let's go." A fireman said calmly, taking her arm without giving her a chance to respond.

"No, wait. I need my rolling pin. I—"

"No time." He whisked her away like she was a feather, obviously used to unreasonable people trying to grab bits of their lives.

"I need my ramekins!" she screamed, and then cried, clutching her purse to her chest as he lifted her off the hardwood floor. As they left the apartment, she heard a horrible noise behind her, a rush, and looked around the brave man's arm to see the ceiling hit the floor, to see fire and smoke begin to fill the room.

Anise spent the night in the emergency room, being checked for smoke inhalation and shock. She wouldn't lift her arm to get her blood pressure checked when asked. She didn't respond to the doctor when asked questions. She shivered, so the nurse put a thin blanket around her slumped shoulders. She didn't speak, but in her mind, a word looped: *Nowhere. Nowhere. Nowhere.* It was difficult to make them understand. It was too complicated for her to articulate. Anise's mind spun so fast it was stationary. She had lost control. She didn't know this, though. She only knew she felt frozen in time and was unable to do or to say. The lights were bright and she was cold. This, she knew.

A Jamaican nurse sat next to her and took her hand, a kind woman, a woman whose lap Anise wanted to curl up on forever, and when Anise looked straight in her eyes, when the woman asked if she had family, she wanted to say, *You*, but after crying a single tear, Anise finally said, "My dad. He's in Buffalo. I've got a dad in Buffalo."

PART III

REPAIRS

A Room of One

She had been fragile these last two years. The familiarity of her dad's old house helped her through. For once, he was able to baby her—at least for two months before he withdrew into his old ways. Anise's first year was one of depression, of spooning chili into her mouth from a can while on the couch, of staring at soap operas, of sleeping during the day. The second year was pulling herself off the couch, lugging herself to the kitchen, cracking an egg into a pan and dragging a fork through it with glazed eyes, squeezing bad, white bread in her fist and whipping it at the wall. At the end of this year, she had a breakthrough: She walked into the aisle of the new grocery store, the one with shiny, dark floors and bulk food, and she scooped flour into a plastic bag. She then found yeast, and before she realized it, she had the ingredients for a simple French bread. She bought good butter and good coffee and took it all home. After she placed two loaves into the oven to rise, she sat in her chair and looked at that old cupboard that held the document, the ancient text, the oracle that had revealed her purpose eons ago. Anise brought her knees to her chin and wrapped her arms around her legs. She closed her eyes and squeezed out a hundred tears for her many losses and pains, and she comforted herself like she did as a child when there was no one else to do it, on nights she was alone, when the house was dark, when her mattress was cold.

Anise took three deep breaths and brought her feet to the floor. Standing up, she kept her eye on the cupboard until she reached it. She was eighteen when she shoved the book in there and banned her mother from her life. Now she was thirty-four. Maybe it wasn't there anymore. Maybe her father tossed it. Realizing that it might be gone forever, she opened the door fast. Cool wind escaped, and gratitude filled Anise. She closed her eyes and cried one more tear. She stood on her toes to see and reached in, taking the cookbook in her hand. She spent the day in the kitchen for the first time in two years. And at some point, though she didn't know when the point began, she realized that though she was not exactly happy, she was, at least, not feeling bad.

****

Standing in front of the tiny building on Elmwood Avenue, Anise found it hard to believe it was hers. She laced her fingers as if in prayer, held her hands to her mouth, took a deep breath, and then fished in her purse for the key.

Once inside, she touched the countertop, the black-vinyl booths. Ripped and sunken. Clearly a diner. But she was a pastry chef so this would be a bakery. A bakery diner. One could have coffee and a danish, a croissant, a cannoli, a sesame ball, a scone. An international bakery. Whatever she felt like making that day. A few things, not too much. Good coffee. She'd be happy, she and her dough, her yeast. Hopefully, she'd cover the costs. Close shop early and rest in the evenings. Rise when it was dark and knead in the quiet. A cat might be nice to keep her company in the back room, which would be her home.

No one would have to know. Looking around the small room, the tiniest eatery in the world, she felt like she finally got what she wanted. She didn't need to make major changes besides a good cleaning, just a little at a time. She needed a glass case for her baked goods and had located one from an old family business that was closing. Sitting in a booth and exhaling, she had the conflicting feelings of both an entrepreneur and a retiree. She had bought it with the savings she amassed while at the hotel. She spent it all.

During the next few weeks, as Anise cleaned and set up her one-room bakery and hidden home in the back, she'd sometimes lose confidence. Up and down Elmwood, storefronts gleamed, their facades shiny and new with beautiful signs. Every detail, perfect. Anise couldn't do that. She didn't paint or draw. She didn't design, and she had no money to hire someone to do it. She baked; that's what she did. So on week four, when she had done the best she could do with what she had, when it was time to open the door because she had to make some money soon, she climbed up a short ladder and nailed a sign above the diminutive façade, below the tiny roof, where the old sign used to be: *Anise's,* painted on an old board in blue and white paint she found in the back. It was crude, and cruder still when she looked up and down the strip. As Anise came down from the ladder, two girls walked by and looked at her shop. They chatted as they continued on, looked behind them and kept going. Anise felt a jolt of nervousness from their interest, realizing she'd soon have real-life customers. At the curb, she sized up her work, snickered. "Oh, well." What she did like though, what tickled her plenty, was the blue, electric word, friendly in loopy cursive: "Bakery." In the little window, it would flash.

Next day, the sight of the neon sign warmed her. The sun was up, too, not quite over the buildings, but the darkness was gone. Her very first day of her very own bakery.

The coffee smelled divine. For her grand opening, she chose *Chocolat Chocolat*, her old favorite. Maybe too sweet to accompany her products, but it was a grand opening, after all. It had to be special, even in the withdrawn approach to life she had groomed.

The door jingled as she sipped coffee with her back to it.

Around she turned, facing a young, professional woman.

Anise had baked for hundreds, perhaps thousands of customers, but the past nine years she had done it from the hotel kitchen, not face-to-face. Anise blushed, spilling her coffee on her red t-shirt.

"Oh, I'm sorry," the woman said. "Did I startle you?"

"Yes. I mean, no. It was my fault. I was in another world." Anise walked quickly to the counter, talking on her way, back in practice as if there hadn't been a lull in her service to others. "What can I get you?" Anise grabbed a sheet of waxed tissue paper and tucked away the desire to be alone. It was easy enough to do; she was a chameleon at the food counter. That was public life. It would cease at five, when the bakery would close, when the blinds would be drawn. Until then, she'd easily take part of the noncommittal relationships forged when exchanging dollars for bread.

"Everything looks delicious." The woman scanned the pastries and breads. "I'll take a lemon tartlet please, and a cup of that coffee. It smells so good."

"Wonderful. Help yourself to the coffee." Anise placed a tartlet in a wax-paper baggie.

On the way out, the woman offered luck for the new business. Anise watched her go. Easy. Smooth. Perfect.

The door opened and two college students walked in.

"What looks good today?" Anise asked.

"Wow, everything," said the blonde boy in faded black jeans, with tattoos on his neck and a silver hoop in one ear. As much as his clothes spoke rebel, his eyes spoke sweetheart, with wide-open blue deference. A pang of something lost forever twitched in Anise's chest. How does she mentally respond to this boy before her? Kiss him or tell him a bedtime story? Anise looked in her case for something to give him.

"How about this?" She held a cherry-cheese Danish on waxed paper.

He blinked. "Oh, yeah. That's it. I'll take it."

She felt her face warm as he examined the delicacy. "Anything else?"

"No, that should do it."

"Great. For here or to go?" Anise stood there, still with the sticky sweet offering in her hand.

He looked around. "I guess for here."

Anise placed the Danish on a paper plate, took his money, and they exchanged smiles as he made his way to a booth.

She took a deep breath, exhaled. "Now. How can I help you?" Anise asked the next boy, this one just a boy like any boy.

The day continued, and with every customer who walked away, cradling one of her treats, she felt the fragile pains within her recede into dormant places.

Homeless Vet #1

Weeks, months, and finally two years passed at *Anise's*. The business bloomed while others around it withered. Anise had a regular customer base that brought in friends who in turn recommended *Anise's*. At times, she had to turn customers away: Large orders would be requested for work parties, but she refused to work overtime. She was a one-woman business, and she knew her limits, and she'd get prickly if pushed past her clearly defined limits. She'd been known to shut the register too hard, to unplug her flashing sign as a customer approached, to turn off the radio right at five, no matter what.

"Time to wake up." The man slumped in Anise's booth didn't stir, so she shook his arm.

He started, eyes red. There was dread in his stare and a sickle-shaped scar under his eye.

"Would you like that cup of coffee?" She figured that was a nice way of asking him to leave.

"Shit, I slept like a log." He came to the present, sat up.

"It's only been fifteen minutes." She responded.

He rubbed gray-brown hands through his hair that was

every which way.

At least he was awake. He had come inside at five-thirty, at dawn; she had made the mistake of unlocking the door early. He had counted out change for coffee, which wasn't enough, sat in a booth and passed out. Early regulars would pop in at six to grab a bite on their way to work. She didn't want him there.

"Cream and sugar?" she asked as she filled a to-go cup.

"Please."

"Here you go."

Anise walked behind her counter and sipped from her mug, wondering how she was going to handle this.

"So what does your day look like?" Anise asked.

"Oh, I've got plenty of prospects." His raspy laugh turned into a coughing frenzy.

Anise winced.

"Excellent blend. My compliments to the barista."

"Compliments accepted."

The door jingled.

Anise beamed too broadly at a woman who had been coming since she opened shop.

"Good morning," Anise said. "You're here early."

"I've got a big day ahead." Pointing with her eyes toward the man, she spoke quietly. "It looks like you do, too."

"Oh, it should be fine," Anise responded, always a pro at detaching. "What looks good today?"

"You don't have any of your twists?" The woman pouted.

"No, I was too busy yesterday to make them. I know they're your favorite." Anise purred. "How about carrot cake?" She pointed to the big squares. "One for now and one for lunch. They are practically right out of the oven."

"Bingo. That's it."

"Great." Anise placed the pieces in individual wax bags.

"You're the best, Anise." The woman headed out,

shooting bug eyes at Anise, tilting her head toward the man in the corner. Conspirators.

Anise had to get him out.

Another regular came in as the woman left—Bill, who lived in an apartment up the street. Bill came in daily, poured himself a cup of coffee, read the paper in the very booth the man was sitting in, and left after an hour. Bill never smiled and didn't talk much. Anise only knew his name because he spoke in third person on his way out. *Bill says thanks for the coffee. Anise says you're welcome* was her quiet response, but he never heard it.

This day, Bill walked in and stood, his loose pants hanging as did his jaw that his booth should be occupied.

"Morning, Bill. How about sitting by the window today?"

He didn't say anything, but tread to the less desirable seat and sat stock-still for three minutes, looking out the window, not getting coffee, not opening his paper.

Both Anise and Bill watched the man walk to the coffee dispenser. The coffee dripped out of the pump-pot, its sound liquid and loud as the three waited. He took his cup back to his seat. Anise breathed. *I can do this.*

"So, what are your *real* plans for today?" Anise tried again.

"Well, I'll probably make my way to the mission."

"Can you sleep there? Can you shower?" Anise immediately wished she could take that back.

"Yeah," he replied, loud and drawn out, "I can do that, but you give up things. When you sleep, someone can take your stuff."

Anise pictured a bag of rags and wondered why anyone would want it.

He seemed to hear her unasked question. "They'll go in your pockets and take your cash. By the time you realize you've been ransacked, the guy is gone."

Anise visualized two homeless men rolling each other.

"I don't steal. That ain't me. My wife married an

87

honorable man. I served in the war—the old war, Nam. No matter what we're fighting for, I don't steal."

Bill rose and walked toward the man. He stood there for a moment, silent.

"9th Infantry Division, 2nd Brigade, Mobile Riverine Force." He put out his hand.

The man wrenched his body out from the booth and stood as straight as he could, taking Bill's hand. Tugging at multiple shirt collars, he revealed a medal dangling from a faded ribbon of yellow, green and red stripes, safety-pinned to his shirt.

Bill nodded. The man gestured for him to sit at the table. Robert was his name. They began a conversation that lasted for two hours. During their time together, the restaurant filled up with college students who didn't think anything at all about the two in the back. Probably, Bill evened it out, brought normalcy to the booth. Likewise, these students evened themselves out, dressing up, dressing down, pairing expensive leather boots with ripped flannel, pierced cheeks with hundred-dollar haircuts.

On the way out, Bill stopped at Anise's counter, dropped his voice.

"We've got to get him some help." He shook his head, "It's not right." He then raised his voice to his usual goodbye octave. "Bill says thanks for the coffee." Out the door he went.

Next morning, Bill was standing on the outside of the restaurant door as she turned the key.

"Morning, Bill."

"I got what we need." He said, grasping a rubber-banded pile of papers.

"What we need?" Anise walked to the counter and Bill followed.

"Where is he?" Bill asked.

"Who?"

"Robert, the guy who needs our help."

"I don't know. The City Mission maybe? I think that's

what he said." Anise was annoyed that she was being brought into this.

Bill smacked the papers on the counter. "Well, it could be worse." He shook his head. "But there's more help to be had." He popped the band and began to unfold papers, some of which looked very old, red and blue ink on thick white paper. "He's served our country. He's got a disfigurement. He should be getting a disability check every month. I know." He served himself coffee. "I was on the phone all day yesterday afternoon." He slurped. "I know these people. I'm at the VA every month. They know me." He spoke with an air of importance that saddened Anise, as if one small man of thousands of vets should have any kind of sway with the government.

"It's almost hard to believe," she said, wiping the counter. "All this time, for all these years, Robert should have been receiving money?"

"Yes!" Bill started coughing. "And no. It's so damn complicated—excuse my French—that nothing ever gets done. You have to prove you were even a vet. And then you have to prove that your cancer—if you have it—is related to Agent Orange. But Robert, he's got the bad leg. That's proof."

"Will he need some kind of papers?"

"Papers!" Bill jerked his back against the booth. "That's all they care about. Papers. But he'll be on record. It's worth the fight—and believe me. It's always a fight."

Anise nodded. She thought this was quite a departure from the pomp she witnessed yesterday, the military pride, but she kept that to herself. "I'm not sure when you'll see him again."

"Let me think about it." He sipped. "I'm a thinker, Anise. I get things done." Bill sloshed some coffee on the counter and looked around as if a magic napkin would fly over and wipe it up.

The door jingled. It was the professional woman, the regular.

"Things back to normal, I see." She flashed a long row of carefully polished teeth.

"More or less," Anise said, disengaging. "Still no twists," Anise stated without apology. She was irritated and tiring quickly of the topic of Robert.

"I suppose I'll have a—what are those called?" She squinted in the direction of a tray.

"Princess Cake."

The woman squealed, dug in her purse, and asked for two slices. Anise quickly placed them in a small paper box. They exchanged money silently. The woman smiled a closed smile and plodded out the door in noisy, heavy shoes.

Anise crossed her arms at her waist.

"I've got an idea!" Bill exclaimed. "I'll drive to the City Mission and find him myself. Would you like to escort an old man tonight?"

God, no. Anise thought. She had a routine, and this wasn't part of it. Though she spoke to people all day long, she didn't spend time with them. She didn't have friends. Her time was her time, and she calculated the hours of the day and night with great care.

"Why do you need me there?" She straightened items on the counter.

Bill played with coins in his pocket and looked down.

"What was I thinking. Forgive me. Why would a busy lady like yourself want to help an old man."

"No, no, that's not it, Bill. I just don't know how I'd help."

"Sometimes us old geezers just don't want to be alone." He cleared his throat. Anise thought about her dad and how she hadn't called him in months.

"Okay, Bill, I'll go. Of course I'll go."

The door jingled.

"Pick you up at seven?"

"That works." *Ugh. There goes sleep.*

At seven on the dot, Bill marched in, smelling of Old Spice. "Bill is ready to go."

Anise was sitting on the edge of a booth and popped up right away, hoping this would take no more than an hour. Out the door they went.

In the car, Anise felt like a child, and she hated it. A passenger, a dependent. She hadn't been in a car in a long time. She crossed her arms. Riding in a long Lincoln, smooth and slow, made the trip feel endless. The driving, out of her control. She took a deep, silent breath and wished she was home.

Downtown now, they approached the mission. For years, Anise had walked the downtown streets as she strutted and loitered with George on her way to the transfer bus back home after school. And years before that, she had shopped with her mother in the department stores, holding her hand, not imagining anything better. Yet, this building on this corner, she never noticed. It wasn't what she had envisioned. When she had heard that word, *shelter*, she pictured beams and boards and unpainted eaves. Yet here was a solid structure of clean bricks, welcoming, a flag at high mast.

Inside the mission, Anise was struck by how orderly everything was. The mission was doing just about everything it could to help the needy—three meals a day, recovery programs, prayer services, showers, beds. Anise didn't know why anyone would have to remain on the street after stopping here.

"We would like to know if you have a man by the name of Robert on your premises." Bill spoke with authority.

"Are you friends or family?" The woman at the counter said.

"Yes, we are exactly that." Bill shoved one hand in his pocket and jangled coins and keys.

"Which?" The middle-aged woman tilted her head covered with puffy, bleached hair.

"Friends, then." Bill sucked his teeth.

"We have a privacy policy. It's up to the guests whether or not they want to share their whereabouts."

Anise spoke up. "Bill here wants to give Robert information about a disability pension he should be getting."

"Do you know his last name?"

No answer.

The woman exhaled. "Wait here." She reached for a set of keys.

Five minutes passed while they sat. Anise read the mission's latest newsletter and Bill clutched his paperwork and smacked his lips.

The woman returned, this time through the door with Robert shuffling behind. His hair was cut and his face was shaven. His clothes were clean and different: a blue sweatshirt and jeans.

"Robert!" Anise blurted, as if they actually were friends.

"In the flesh," he replied, still missing teeth.

"I didn't recognize you." Anise stated. "You look great."

"Well, Robert. It looks like you're on the right track." Bill addressed his war buddy as if things were unfolding as they should, as if Robert had made the right choice and the universe was rewarding his efforts. "I've got disability paperwork for you to fill out. I can take you to the VA tomorrow to get this going."

"That would be great." The woman dropped her shoulders, relief in her face. "Robert's been working on this for quite a while."

"He has?" Anise asked.

"Oh, yes." She patted Robert's shoulder. "We've been friends for years."

Robert snickered. "One day at a time." He shook his head.

Anise scanned the room. Was she the only one who

felt the weight of that statement?   Bill said nothing. Anise knew at that moment that Robert would always be on the street.   The broken would always be broken, no matter what anyone did.

Back in the car, Bill and Anise drove away from the shelter. Anise let the wash of downtown recede as she put her head back on the sun-faded leather. There were better ways to spend her time than on people who refused to help themselves while organizations, old men and bakers were going out of their way.

Homeless Vet #2

Days passed since Anise and Bill had visited Robert. Bill had gone back to the mission the next day but Robert wasn't there. Bill continued to come to his booth in the mornings but was fidgety as he read the paper, would look up every time the door jingled. This morning he left without his usual announcement.

It was a sunny afternoon. Customers were content. Anise sipped coffee and looked out the window, noticing dirty spider webs in the sun, on the outside. She grabbed a rag and stepped out for a moment and began to wipe away the mosquito-carcasses that floated in the breeze. She paused in her wiping and glanced at a man who was about to pass. He wore an army jacket and jeans and carried a cardboard sign: HOMELESS VET. ANY HELP WOULD BE APPRECIATED. She slapped the rag at the corners of the window. *Not another one.* Homeless vets were coming out of the woodwork.

"Mornin'," he said.

"Morning," she returned, still slapping as he walked by. He was younger than Robert—too young to be out on the streets, to not be working. Might even be attractive—it was hard to tell through the facial hair and hat pulled over his eyes. "Why the hell is he homeless?" she asked quietly. She didn't get it, not this one. Wasn't he supposed to be one of our heroes? How do you get from there to here? From the photos in the paper, the strong, the shaven, young men, ready to save the world? She shook her head. He was halfway down the block when she mentally clothed him in clean fatigues, gave him a buzz cut, straightened his back. Yet here he was—shunned? Forgotten? Lazy? Whose fault was this?

"Excuse me," Her voice was too quiet. She repeated it, louder this time. "Excuse me, sir?"

He turned.

"Would some food help?" *How stupid is that?* Her rag hung from her fingers.

"It couldn't hurt," he said and stepped toward her.

"I'll be right out," she said, setting the boundaries.

Inside, she snatched a lemon danish from the case and bagged a loaf of olive and rosemary bread. She brought it outside.

"Here you are," she said triumphantly, as if she just changed his life.

"Thank you, ma'am." The bearded man replied, reaching out for the items with darkened, thick fingers.

"Ma'am? I'm not *that* old."

"You're older than me." His legs shook a little as he held the food.

"You can sit here if you'd like."

"Awesome, thanks." The vagrant sat down, his boots curled in, his shoulders hunched.

Back inside, seeing his shabby appearance through the window, she regretted offering him a seat. He might start coming all the time, ruining business. She wiped the counter, smiled at a customer. Distracted by his presence as she worked, she dropped a tray of Napoleons on the floor, making a loud bang that was heard through the open window. Outside, the vet jumped up from his moment of afforded entitlement, looked her way in terror, and traipsed off.

Sweeping up the broken mille-feuille, its flaky layers and custard filling having spread like a dropped deck of cards, Anise mumbled, in a private war, first berating herself for her condescension, then sticking up for herself because it wasn't her job to change his world; she was doing her best just to take care of herself, *thank you very much*.

For days, Anise saw no sign of the man and didn't think about him either. She liked her routine, and vets had disturbed it. On Mondays through Saturdays, she was wedded to the establishment, except for the occasional sprint to the corner store or the library in the evening. On Sundays, her only day off, she ran errands and got caught up on paperwork. Down the block was the Laundromat, and she'd routinely wash two loads, light and dark, and read while the washers pulsated. Vegetable and cheese shopping was done at the co-op up the block; salads and cheese (and her pastry and bread) were her mainstay. Her routine worked; a bump in it could screw up everything she built.

Weeks went by. One Sunday morning, very early, not quite dawn, Anise sat on her bench in front of the bakery with her eyes closed, a cup of coffee in her hand, the first time doing this ever. Hearing a shuffling gait, she opened her eyes.

The man teetered a bit, looked dry, scorched. "Are you gonna ask me to sit down?"

Shit. Anise scooted over without saying a word.

"Beautiful morning." He said.

"Yes, I guess it is."

"I *know* it is."

Anise exhaled. "Did you like the danish?"

"It was great, thanks."

"And the bread?"

"It was…good." He looked up the street.

"Good, you say."

"I'm not really an *olive* fan."

"Hmph." Anise's response was barely audible but heard.

"I know. I'm supposed to be grateful for what I get."

She didn't respond but thought, *yeah, that's right.*

"I wasn't always on the street." He sat back. One dry and cracked hand lay palm-up on the bench between them.

She wished he could just pull himself together and face life. She had made a life for herself with no help at all. She saw how Robert held on to his misery, despite everyone willing to help. *Get with the program*, she wanted to say to these men.

She decided she'd send him on his way with a goodbye-coffee. "Would you like some coffee?"

He stared at the ground. "All right."

Anise headed in and realized that he took the door from her and followed. She closed her eyes for a moment. How long would he stick around?

"I'm not open today, so this will just be a fill-and-go."

Inside, the lights were off, and she was uneasy that they were alone. Anise flicked on a light over the counter, turned around, and there he stood.

Four hours later, the man named Pete fell asleep, head in her lap. It was time to ask him to leave. The heaviness of his story weighed on her. She needed water. She needed air. Oh, sure, her customers—some more than others—would share highlights of their lives. But she had never heard a confession, had never petted a matted head, had never felt the shaking of a crying, younger man. She stared into space and wondered how this happened.

"Pete?" Her voice was soft, perhaps too soft, so she repeated it. "Pete?"

He slept soundly. Perhaps it was a good sleep, not one riddled by gunfire. She didn't have the heart to wake him to go back to his stash, to his current spot, one of the many boarded up homes on the other side of Main Street.

Freeing her legs from his head and shoulders, she rose, stretching away stiffness.

There he lay with no blanket or pillow on a linoleum bakery floor. This was his life. In her room, she grabbed a blanket, one of the two she owned, and placed it over his slumbering body, first taking in the wormy veins and sculpting of his arms. He had finally taken off his jacket, not wanting to, discomfited by his own smell, but Anise demanded he do it because of the heat. He must have been handsome, she thought, and it pained her that she thought of him in past tense.

It was still morning, but she was exhausted from being attentive to someone besides herself. She retreated to her haven, locked the door. Her cat, Mandy, purred. Anise had made a lovely room for herself these past years. A futon, a colorful lamp, a rug, her books, her clothes hanging in a painted broom closet. She had replaced the old basin with a new sink and counter. Off that room was her own shower, too, purchased and installed with the last of her saved dollars.

Though it was too early to sleep, she did. In the early evening, she woke to find Pete gone, blanket on the floor and the door wide open. She shivered at her vulnerability. She shut the door, locked it, and quickly made her way to the register and sighed, relieved that it had been untouched. Still, she rubbed her arms and scurried to the windows, closed the blinds, and she was safe.

Anise put on coffee and tied back her hair. It was too early to bake, but it would relax her if she did. She washed her hands, popped in her Modern English CD quietly, an old favorite, so no one would hear but her. She wrapped a stained white apron around her waist and began to bake. She had all the time in her safe world.

And it began, the soft maelstrom.

It would be marzipan.

She first knew marzipan in an almond ring, years back,

as a child. Technically, that was almond paste. The ring would be on the list of items she was to pick up from Wilson's the morning after. Her father would be lying on the sofa, smoking and sallow, and this would be breakfast. At age eleven, shopping was an easy task. Back home from the store, she'd cut the tight cellophane with a steak knife, and then she'd cut herself a wedge and eat it standing, exhaling. After stirring instant coffee into a cup, she'd walk the cup and a big wedge of pastry on a small plate to the living room and lower breakfast to Carl. In the kitchen, another piece for her with milk, and she'd be set until dinner. Inside the dough of the ring, the almond paste was the best part, sweet and gooey. The dough was dry, but there was white sugar frosting on top with slivered almonds. Anise knew that without the dry dough, the moist paste wouldn't be as good, and in the same respect, it was fitting that without the hangover, there would be no almond ring.

At culinary school and beyond, marzipan was marzipan—or was it? It was forever debated amongst the creators, across continents, the best, true recipe. Still, one thing all renditions contained was a mash of almonds and sweetness. This concoction, or its sister, almond paste, Anise sneaked in every flaky crevice she could.

From the refrigerator, she scooped into her palms marzipan dough that she had made the day before.

As she rolled her almond and sugar dough into balls, her head swam with vivid memories Pete had shared, only bits and pieces that he could verbalize. Stone-faced, he had said, looking past Anise to the wall as they had sat in the booth, "It's almost better not to live. I'm back there anyway." Staring at the tabletop he had said, "Sounds are bad," and he looked over to the kitchen, "and smells." She had questioned with her eyes. "It's good you're not cooking meat, Anise. I couldn't sit here. Cooked flesh is cooked flesh."

It was talking about the children that caused him to roll

to the floor. "Little kids." And he covered his face, "I didn't know," he had squealed, "I didn't know."

Anise had mothered him, shushed him.

Now covered with sweet dough, her marzipan balls would soon be cookies.

Four pecan pies would be next, followed by custard tartlets. After that, the bread.

She placed a full sheet of cookies in the big oven. Before continuing, she reached up to change her CD. Above the CD player, a red gingham cookbook was on display, though no one ever remarked on it, just as no one would remark on a tablecloth or a light fixture. Sometimes, Anise thought she would hear the pages ruffle.

Challah. Lots of challah—thirty-six braids, six loaves. Three poppy, three plain, all eggy sweetness. Anise placed the bulky yellow loaves on the racks behind her, then from the second oven that was warm she seized four long, savory bread loaves, olive and basil, covered in white cotton and ready to bake. Removing the cloths, she put the loaves in the next oven, still hot from the challah. During the forty minutes they would bake, she mixed quick-bread batter, adding juicy peaches that were in season, and making lemon sour-cream too. That was plenty. Into the second oven they went. The sky was still dark; she was ahead of schedule. She would lie down again when the ovens were empty. Mandy would curl up with her. It would be peaceful.

Anise scraped flour off the counter, washed the bread pans, and soon, everything was out of the oven and cooling. She untied her apron. It was time to wash up.

Damp and clean, wearing an olive-green t-shirt and black leggings, she lay down, setting her alarm. Her body clock was off. She could sleep forever.

Days and weeks passed, and Anise saw no sign of Pete. Each day was easier to forget he ever entered her life. Even so, their brief encounter would find its way into her thoughts as she baked in the wee hours. She would see his taut arm in the elastic dough she stretched, would hear his whimper in the buzz of the timer.

Six months passed and all was back to normal. Almost. Problem was, she had felt him vibrate in her lap from the barrage of blasting from his past, had heard shattered bits of his story. So when she caressed the books on the library shelves, and folded her laundry in the Laundromat, and walked past the psychiatric center on her way to the art gallery, she saw him. He'd be on the computer in the library, in the form of an elderly, bearded man. He'd be talking to himself in the Laundromat, in the form of a padded, black man. He'd be picking at his face on the corner, in the form of a young man who had lost his mind.

"Hey, Anise. Coffee's empty!" One of three college boys announced. Anise turned from her thoughts to see who was calling. It was Derek, the one who drank more than he spent. The one who was blonde and adorable, with eyebrows that rose as if he was saying, *I can't help it. Can you help?*

"I'm on it."

Adding the coffee to the pot, she listened to the laughter and ruckus in the booth by the window. Would these boys consider joining the army? They were too beautiful, too happy, as far as she could see. They had too much ahead of them. There had to be a better way of making the world a better place than by destroying the ones who did the work.

Turning from the coffee station, Anise looked at the door and in walked Pete. Weird, how the mind plays tricks. During these months, Anise had transformed him into something different, something more handsome, taller, cleaner—perhaps the man she imagined he had been. Now he just looked like a bum, a vagrant who shouldn't be inside, bugging the customers who had paid money for food and who should not be bothered.

Anise walked quickly to the counter so Pete wouldn't get closer to the customers.

"I was just thinking about you," Anise said as she made her way behind the counter, striking a clear boundary.

"Really? And what were you thinking?" He coughed into his sleeve. He didn't look good up close, either. His eyes were red, and she could smell beer on his breath. He teetered a bit.

"I was thinking," she searched for words, "I was hoping you were okay." And she looked down and straightened pens near the register.

"Hey, I am A-OK." He smiled, and his darkened teeth revealed his daily trials. From a bag he carried on his shoulder, he fished out two dollar bills and a bunch of change. "For coffee." He slid the money toward her. He ambled to the one empty booth without getting coffee and sat with one leg hanging out. Anise gathered the money and filled a cup full of coffee and brought it to him, and though she was about to return the money to him, she thought it might be an insult or an embarrassment, so she kept it tight in her hand and walked back to the register. Once there, it dawned on her that it wasn't too embarrassing for him to hold up a sign and ask for money, so maybe he would accept this money without a problem. Exasperated with worrying over the ego of this man, she popped open the register and shoved the money in its proper compartments and slammed it closed.

One booth over from Pete, a woman chewed slowly, her young daughter beside her. She watched Pete, her eyes calculating the situation as he coughed into his sleeve. Gathering her things—purse, shopping bags, kindergartner—she hustled out the door.

"Great." Anise said to herself, arms stretched out, hands gripping the counter edge.

It was six o'clock in the evening and the restaurant was closed. Pete had fallen asleep in the booth. She had been afraid to wake him earlier and cause commotion.

"Pete, time to wake up." She tried not to touch him so that he wouldn't jump, but her voice was getting nowhere, so she patted his arm. "Pete. Wake up."

He stirred. He opened one eye and peered at her. Without speaking, he began to scoot out of the booth when his bag hit the floor. Anise bent down and picked it up.

"Ugh, this is heavy—"

"I'll take that." He snatched it from her.

"Sorry, I was just—"

"Yeah, thanks." And out he went.

Anise watched him leave, slinging the weighted bag over his shoulder with ease. His posture was erect, his stride, determined. Mentally, she again clothed him in uniform, could see his honor, his shaved cheeks, his loyalty. And what was his mission now?

In the bag, she had thought she heard glass rattling, maybe something heavier. Metal?

Locking up, she lugged her tired body to her room. She needed sleep. She always needed sleep. Reaching out to the world was exhausting—emotionally and physically. She was happy to be back in her cocoon. Safe, predictable. After opening the back door so Mandy could go outside, she removed her old sandals and collapsed on the futon. Her mouth hung open, and her imagination took over, truth found in dreams.

Anise's dreams were always a wash—a watercolor swirl that she'd have a hard time remembering. She would only remember one piece of the very last dream before waking, and just like that, the watercolor swirl would wash away, like a pastel Etch-a-Sketch being shaken. Sometimes she'd try to grasp at it, and sometimes it would leave so quickly she wouldn't even remember that she dreamed.

Her dream this night begins with water, and her mother, and her father. This dream is a regular dream, and because of that, unremarkable. It is part of her, and in fact, part of her reality. This dream is never in pastels, but in cold, dark colors.

After that dream, pastels usually enter. They might be pink fondant or lemon strudel. Whatever the case, it is always a pleasant entry in her wash of dreams. If she dreams of such things this night, they are forgotten.

This night, warm reds and yellows make their appearance. There is an epic quality to it, *Gone with the Wind*, or some such family saga. Anise's face is by this time on her pillow, drool spilling.

It is a big room, one of many, with high ceilings, marble and rococo. Down the winding staircase Felice sashays, Felice of cooking school, of many brothers and friends. Down she parades, a tall, hot-pink toque on her head, dark curls flowing, a chef's jacket of the same hue but with no pants—instead, black hosiery. One great thigh lifts, then another. The watercolor wash swirls slightly and flowers fill Felice's arm. A violent swirl, and she is tumbling down the stairs! At the bottom of the steps she sits, her toque askew. In pain and glaring up the stairs, she sees a small face peering, a giggle hidden behind a hand. The little vixen has pushed her! Felice gets her bearings and stomps up the stairs, ready to strangle her naughty offspring who *ruins everything!*

A shake of the dream powder and Felice is at her grand table, serving. Here, she is composed, serene, clothed. Daughter looks up to her in admiration. Anise turns on her side, yanks up the blanket. Her dream's camera pulls back quickly, quicker, and the grand table is never-ending, laden with countless dishes and surrounded by countless family members who all smile—no, wait, not true! The camera slows and some are not smiling. Some are arguing. Some have divorced. Some have been unfaithful and have hives on their necks. A teenager snorts cocaine—there, on the table. A toddler scoots next to the teen and snorts too, and Anise scowls, both in the dream and in bed. She screams in her dream, but her scream is muffled, soundless. *No!*

Anise turns to leave, to run, but her pace is deadened, her pace is like caramel, and the foyer lengthens as she goes. People begin to appear on either side. An old widow wearing a black mantilla stares but sees nothing. Anise looks a second longer and sees it is Gino's mother, and there is Gino by her side who reaches for Anise, but Anise is too far away. Two of Felice's brothers toss buttered rolls to one another, but one brother is Gino's rebellious son who whips a roll at Gino. Anise reaches for the roll, but the Statue of David appears and looms over Anise. Something is awry. He is missing his penis! Across the marble floor, Anise sees the severed member and scurries to it. Holding it in her hand, she scuttles back and tries desperately to fit it in place, but alas, it will not hold. Still, she continues to try to affix the shaft until she realizes she is surrounded by the clan. When she sees them, they burst out laughing, louder and louder. Anise shakes her head, tries to explain herself over the mirth, but cannot be heard, and when she begins to cry, they come forward, comforting her, telling her she brought them joy. Gino claws through all of them and holds her arms firmly in her hands. *We are family!* He says. *We are family!* Anise is escorted to the table. She cries, looking side to side at these people who bring her into their fold.

Crying, Anise woke on her stomach. This dream, she remembered.

She sat up, rubbing her head. The watercolors had been bright shades. The family had been vivid. They weren't perfect. There's was full of problems. But family is family, and she had been included in it. She was brought to the table.

Anise had a table that needed to be set. Her offerings were made alone in the dark and handed out in the light one at a time in bits and bites. But there was another formula, and with all these years and experience of food preparation, she had yet to run the program, to test the flowchart. This, she needed to do, if only just once. She needed to bring her family to her.

She looked at the clock. 11:02 PM. Time to bake for her customers tomorrow and to begin planning a spring banquet.

Cost of a Meal

During Anise's month of banquet preparation, she noticed a decrease in business. Women who had been regular patrons, those with toddlers and presumptions, stopped coming. Others, too. Pete, though, was stopping by every day, now that he had moved his belongings to a closer, safer place. He was doing more than stopping by—he was arriving in the morning, taking his place in the back, and staying for hours.

Bill had been coming as usual and would sit with Pete and try to convince him to fight the system, to go after what was rightfully his, to file a claim. Pete would nod and return Bill's pleas with vague replies and eventually no replies at all, which finally compelled Bill to sit at another booth. Even Bill had a threshold.

Anise felt she was doing her part to be family as best she could, letting Pete slump in the booth, giving him free coffee and danish, talking with him, patting his arm as she headed off. She'd make a joke to see if he still knew how to laugh, and when he'd crack a smile or respond with sarcasm, she'd go back to work, relieved that he was still in touch. But he was getting less and less responsive. Sometimes, he'd just stare at the wall and not talk at all.

He smelled like beer, and she caught him more than once taking swigs from a can he kept hidden. She let it go, turned her eye. He was broken, and looking into his red eyes that contrasted with the soft patch of his cheeks above his beard, she had the idea that some people just can't handle their brokenness, that if you break enough, all you can do is simply carry on.

Robert, the first homeless vet in Anise's life, had popped in twice during the month, not drinking and smelling nice, and she thought that his efforts, in comparison, were analogous to a sober man holding down a job. A day without a drink was a victory, and if he should have one morning when he might look at his reflection, look into the cracking of his iris, into the pain and loneliness, yet still bring the razor to his chin, knowing the hair would just sprout again, he had triumphed.

One day, toward the end of the month, the month that flew by, the month that Anise was sleeping even less than usual, gathering recipes and ingredients for her banquet, making place cards, placing orders for flowers and duck, on this day, she was cashing out a customer when she noticed that Pete was not even hiding his beer can. There it sat, in front of him, and he lifted it and gulped.

Her eyes widened, which caused a customer she was cashing out to turn and look.

"What'dja expect?" he asked, "Give 'em an inch and they'll walk all over you."

Anise watched the customer leave, wondered if he'd ever come back. She closed the register and made her way to Pete and sat across from him. She was hesitant, as his demeanor had been getting more and more withdrawn and unpredictable.

"Pete, I know I've been turning my eye on this." She gestured to the can, like a conductor. "But I could get in trouble."

"Not a problem." He seemed to snap out of a trance. "Besides, the weather's getting nicer." He reached for his bag.

"Pete." She touched his jacketed arm. "Just don't drink here anymore, okay?"

"I hate to tell you this, but if it's a choice, I pick this." He lifted up the can.

Anise didn't have it in her to throw her body in front of him. She knew that Pete thought he hadn't a family to go to, that his mother was married to some "new guy" she met while Pete was in Iraq. And his dad left when he was a young child. His sister and her family, who lived in the suburbs, he didn't want to bother. He never spoke of a girlfriend, and being a loner, Anise never thought of asking.

"Please come to my dinner party, okay? It's for the regulars. It's my one big bash."

"I'll check my calendar." Pete grabbed his bag in one hand. He walked past her and out the door.

The eatery was now empty. She looked at her glass case and the bread shelves; they were almost full even though it was three o' clock. At this time of the day, she'd usually have a rush but there was no one. She had to admit, the place smelled of Pete, not completely, but it did. Even Bill didn't seem too happy lately; he had left earlier than usual all week. Slumped in the booth, she changed seats, took Pete's spot, assessed the situation. She realized that she had been so caught up in her planning—had even dipped into her register more than once, that she had failed to notice the extent of the change of her customer base. The week had been so light—she had been thankful—but now she realized the month might be ending on a sour note. Her budget was a monthly one: electricity and supplies mostly. She dreaded looking at the numbers, but she was one to face reality even in the face of hardship, even in the face of her own carelessness.

It was Pete, his presence, that was doing this. Could one man that no one wanted to deal with, who wouldn't even deal with himself, cause a business to collapse?

Instead of facing the numbers, she faced the wall he had looked at every day for the past month. The booth was warm. It smelled like body odor, stale beer and cigarettes from the many breaks he took during the day. She looked under the table. Crumbs. She looked at the dingy wall—one of the things she didn't tend to, she now realized. Other than food, she hadn't thought about the customers' needs. She had a sinking feeling it was too late.

Anise picked at the vinyl of the booth and thought of the few things Pete had shared about his life as a boy. He had mentioned hockey—he liked to play ice hockey and street hockey. He was good, but he'd let his sister score a goal sometimes because otherwise, she would have quit.

Pete had shown her his photos he kept in a black wallet, and in one, he is sitting in a dangerous high-chair. A man's wrist is captured in the photo, holding the spoon. Baby Pete doesn't look at the spoon in the photo but only gazes at the masculine feeder.

Anise put her head in her arms on the table and thought of her own father who she had been calling every night this month. She could call him or not call him—a day, a year could pass—and he'd say the same thing: "Hey, Cookie." Whether she should laugh or cry, she didn't know. Whether it was unconditional love or that he gave up on her, or if it was that she was just another channel on the TV, she didn't know. She thought of Pete's noncommittal ways brought on by too much of one thing—horror—and she decided to finally go with that option, that the one thing her dad had too much of was her mother.

"If he only knew," she said into her arm.

Anise lifted her head. Or did he know? Did he suspect something but refuse to believe? When she had put the pieces together, even *she* could figure it out, and she wasn't married to him. *She was never satisfied, it seemed. She might be next to us on the couch, watching TV, but her mind was someplace else.* "He thought he married Mother

Theresa." Anise peeled a strip of vinyl clear off the seat, exposing rotting yellow foam.

Her father would be at the party. He had said yes. That was something. She gained solace in that.

And then there was George. Her dear George, who she had thought of inviting but was afraid. She sat up straight in the booth and chewed her nails. Maybe he would be indifferent, like her dad, like Pete. But wasn't it worth the risk? Wasn't this it, her gathering, her one shot at tying together some of what she lost? Didn't her dream tell her what she had to do?

Really, Anise thought, as she stood in front of the bakery and locked it, closing early, George was better off without contact from her. It would complicate things, confuse him. While thinking about this on her way to the library, she jumped in her skin because the sky, which had been darkening quickly the last hour, cracked open with startling thunder. A sheet of rain rushed down like a massive curtain at the end of a performance. She had never seen that before: the point where water enters air.

Through wet eyes, she walked and ran down the blocks. Two roguish men in a beat-up car rode by.

"Hey, need a ride, sweetheart?" one bellowed, rolling down his window.

She glanced at the car. Both men wore grins. She saw herself in their eyes: wet leggings and t-shirt, hair hanging in soggy ropes, desperation.

Even the wayward find her needy. Running to revive a memory.

And really, how desperate she would appear to George. How pathetic, she thought. Searching the internet for a high-school friend because she didn't have any. She wiped water off her face with her fingers and flicked it to the sidewalk. Inside the library, she carried her heavy self, a drenched woman who used the library for computer access because she *had* to. Who portioned vegetables to last a week. Who slept secretly in the back of a restaurant.

Things that had seemed commendable at one time she saw differently in that moment—through the eyes of two laughing men who had a car, who kept dry in the rain, who had each other.

The library had always brought peace. It was her church, a place she'd go for refreshment, for quiet, to light a candle—to pull a book from a shelf, admire the heft of it, the careful cataloging, the photo of the author, and then place it back in its spot, just happy it was there.

Today, though, she went straight to the bank of computers. Patrons were only allowed one hour a day. George's coordinates were possibly at her fingertips. Or she might not find him at all, she thought, as she logged into the system. Into the search engine, she typed his full name in quotes. Many pages of possibilities appeared.

For twenty minutes, she found Georges, but not the right one. Then she found a possibility on a social networking site. "Ugh." To access him, she'd have to join. After subscribing, she clicked on this George's account, this George who lived in Chicago. "He stayed," she said aloud, remembering that he had attended an art college, that he even wanted her to visit, a million years ago.

The picture surprised her: A grown-up, a man, one with wrinkles and wisdom. And he was thin. "My George," she said quietly, truly happy to see how wonderful he looked, how content, at least from the photo. His page hadn't been visited in over a year. His marital status, however, was clearly marked: married. "I see," she said, and exhaled. Off limits. A lost opportunity. Even if she just wanted to be friends, how would his wife feel about a long-lost, seemingly desperate woman from his past contacting him?

But what did she have to lose?

Typing an email, she began:

> *Hey, you! Remember me? It's Anise, from yesteryear. How are you? It's been so incredibly long. I see that you*

are married. Congratulations! I truly wish you the best.
You look wonderful (from your MySpace photo).

 I was originally searching for you to see if you'd be able
to come to a spring banquet I'm throwing at my restaurant.
Yes, restaurant—well, a bakery (a teeny one). Remember
when I forced you to cook with me? Ha-ha! Well, I never
stopped. And I'm throwing this party, but, alas, I see you
do not live in Buffalo any longer. Boo-hoo. It would have
been great to see you. If there is any chance you're in town
next week, the party is on May 1st. Look for Anise's on
Elmwood, okay? Near Auburn, the library, that area. I
would love to see you there! Bring your wife, too. The more
the merrier!

She didn't want to say that last part, but it seemed the
right thing, to show her intentions were honorable.

 She sent the email. She left the library and walked
slowly back home in the rain, feeling both light and heavy.

Spring Banquet

Anise experienced the same psychological rush she experienced years ago, at the Valentine Luncheon she prepared for her dad, for herself, for George, the meal that made George leave her. Though she had been baking for people for years, she hadn't prepared a table since culinary school. And though Anise appreciated her bread and pastry life, it still existed in a vacuum, in an economy; in fact, it was her bread and butter. Years had gone by since she had eaten a meal with anyone at all. Not even lunch at a café. Sitting over coffee wasn't the same. This, she realized, as she folded mismatched cloth napkins into birds of paradise (she had bought them at The Salvation Army along with an iron, all for $7). It was one of her great losses, this lack of eating meals with people, she concluded, as she placed another bird on a booth table.

Humans act strange if left alone too long. Eating together at a table with chairs and silverware civilizes a person. If one eats cross-legged on one's futon for too many days, for too many years, one starts to cry, to rock in one's place, to not bother washing bowls, to stack dishware alongside one's bed and stare at the wall.

Formal dinners create courtesy, manners, respect and

even love—it said so in the cookbook she had been reading again.

She had closed early, and the duck was delivered at three o'clock. The main course would be Duck a l'Orange. She cheated and used duck breasts only. It would be a little tricky, because best results required searing right before serving, ten minutes each side, hot off the stove. Nine guests were invited. She would make it work by having three or four burners going at once. She'd have to cook the main course instead of mingling, but everyone would be happy, chatting, and eating h'orderves that consisted of:

> -*gougères* (cheese puffs (though in France, you'd eat cheese closer to the main course))
> -*salade jambon melon* (ham & melon)
> -*pâté rustique* (Anise did not buy this pate but made it herself, mincing veal and pork, and though no one would ever confirm this, she knew it had to be the most delicious pate in all of the United States, at least)
> -French bread (perfect, of course)
> -*apéritifs* (Kir)

As she set her mismatched china (incredible bargain) on the cloth-covered booths, all her work and preparation became reality. She could hear the conversations already, could see her dad popping a cheese puff in his mouth while nodding to Bill's diatribe. She could see the illuminated walls ($10 for two lamps) as her four regular students took on the sophistication of the room, talking seriously about their ambitions, getting ready to start their adult lives. Pete would chat—hand in his jacket pocket— with Robert, who would tell him how it's tough, but nights like this give you hope. And cutting into tender duck, she could see George's disbelief, as he shook his head, that this night was actually happening. And finally, she could see her awareness, as she opened her napkin on her lap, that it almost didn't happen, and she would feel a flood of gratitude that it was. She would then ask herself, as she looked at a gray hair in George's mustache, *Why, oh why didn't I do this sooner?*

The side dishes were all done and warm in the oven: *céleri rémoulade*, the cheesy *aligot*, and individual spinach soufflés served in new ramekins.

The dessert was set in eleven individual, stemmed glasses of various designs (25-to-50 cents, depending), in honor of a distant memory: Orange Fig Whip.

Anise had gone in her backroom to get ready. A second-hand dress. The dress, she knew, was the one. It was a dress with yellow flowers, a dress from an earlier age, something she could see her mother admiring but never wearing. The weather was really too cool for it, but from this dress she determined her floral décor for the room: yellow flowers of all kinds, everywhere.

At 6:45, fifteen minutes before guests were due to arrive, she began to light candles that were on each of three booths—four people would sit in two booths, two people in a third. She didn't know where to stand or sit to wait for people; her place had always been behind the counter, but today, these weren't customers. She decided to take her stool that she kept behind the counter and bring it around to the other side—hostess like.

By 7:00, when still no one had come, she adjusted table settings. Finally, at 7:05, she went behind the counter and stared out the window.

She inhaled as her dad pulled up in front. As she watched him get out of the car, she was touched by how clean and dressed up he was—dressed up for him: a patterned, button-down shirt and his "good" jeans. In the door he walked, filling the space with his familiar presence.

"Hey, Cookie," he said. "Am I early?"

"No, you're late," she said, "and by the looks of it, it might be just us."

"Well, that wouldn't be so bad, would it?" he said, his

hair now almost completely gray, the hanging skin on his jaw painful to see.

"No, not at all," she said, not completely honest. "How about an appetizer?" She led him to the counter, showed him the array of goodies.

"You've outdone yourself. You tell me. Which one should I try first?"

"For you, the gougères, AKA, cheese puff." Anise waved her hand in front of the platter.

"Cheese puff is right." Carl popped one in his mouth, then chewed while he spoke. "Best cheese puff I ever had."

"Only cheese puff you've ever had."

"That, too."

The door jingled.

Looking over her shoulder, she was greeted by her four students, headed by her favorite, Derek, the blonde who drank too much of her coffee, who was having a hard time getting through his classes, who had probably been diagnosed with ADHD in his childhood, who might not make it through college, but who was brilliant.

"Whoa," he said, backing up in exaggerated surprise, bumping into his entourage. "Awesome, Anise."

The party was official. No matter what happened now, no matter who else arrived, it was here, and she made it happen.

She directed the young men to the h'orderves, made aperitifs for everyone, turned on some background music, choosing the classical station for this night, and began to sear duck.

Everyone showed but Pete and George, but she was okay because the room was alive. Pete probably couldn't bring himself to attend something that required a commitment, and George, well, who knew if he even got the message. She had gone to the library and checked her email during the week and there had been no response. Chances were slim that either would show, but she wasn't going to wallow there when before her were enough people to make her believe that she did have a family of sorts. She lifted a tray of duck a l'orange and headed toward the booths.

The door jingled.

Anise turned to see. At first, she didn't recognize the man who stood there. His beard was gone and his hair was cut short. "Pete! You look wonderful!" She said, holding the tray. "Come sit with Robert and Bill." She gestured with her head. "And my dad, you have to meet my dad."

As Pete walked closer, she realized he had been drinking. She tried to blink away her disappointment and let him make his way to the booth himself so that she didn't drop the tray. She served the students first, stealing a glance in Pete's direction. The boys were just as she hoped: mannerly, appreciative of what was being set before them, and when Derek looked up at her, there was something different in his countenance, and whether it was the look of a son or a lover she couldn't discern—maybe there was a little of both as he glanced at the neckline of her dress and the color on her lips—but either way, it didn't matter because there was love in the room, and she made it happen.

Anise returned to the stove and placed four duck breasts on the platter when she heard voices at the older men's table getting louder, rowdier. Bringing the platter to the table, everything seemed okay, just a sudden outburst. She placed an entrée on each plate. Bill was a gentleman as was Robert who looked tired and maybe a day after a binge, maybe ready to be repentant again and start anew. Her dad looked at the duck and said, "Well, now." Pete stared into Anise's face, and though she saw his inability to focus, she didn't see his inward plea for understanding. She didn't see that in order to get to her place, he had spent the previous night at the shelter. That he had carried her invitation in his pocket all month. That he washed his clothes and wished he could shine his boots. That he wanted to tell her that he was grateful for her ears and her eyes, for the soft hand on his arm, and for her soft lap that he remembered. That it had been the only physical tenderness he had experienced in two years, but things were just too far gone, and there was no coming back.

"Well, what d'ya think?" Pete asked, his eyes on Anise.

"I think you look incredibly handsome."

"I'll take that," he said.

Anise went back to the kitchen and pulled the warm side dishes out of the oven. She brought them to the booths.

"Anise, come, sit down," Carl said.

"I will, I will."

Pete pulled a beer can out of his bag and popped it open. There was silence at the table as he chugged.

"Pete, come sit at this booth with me." Anise had set up a booth for her and George.

"Yeah, yeah, okay, send the drunk away." Pete got up from his seat, carrying his can, placing it on Anise's table and going back for his dishes. She gave a look to her father to put him at ease.

"So, how does your spinach soufflé look?" He looked at his plate, trying to locate the soufflé. "Yeah, sure, it looks good."

"Take a bite. Tell me if you like it," she said, cutting into her duck, placing it into her mouth.

Obediently, he scooped a forkful of yellow and green substance from his ramekin and stuck it in his mouth.

"What do you think?" She took a bite. "I made it just for you."

"For me? Then why are all these other people eating *my soufflé?*" he joked, but it was abrasive.

"Now, now, you've got to be able to share, Pete."

He put his fork down, gulped his beer.

"Try this." She ladled the thick and creamy *aligot* onto his plate.

He sipped his beer, put down the can, placed a spoonful of *aligot* in his mouth as if he were doing her a favor. His expression changed. "Good." He ate all that was on his plate and continued to empty the serving bowl of the potato and cheese comfort food onto his plate as well. "Got any more?"

"Actually, I do." Happy he was filling his stomach, she took the serving bowl to the kitchen and filled it with more, humming all the while.

"Oh," she exclaimed, bumping into him as she turned, not realizing he had followed her. It was doubly strange because she never had anyone behind the counter. "You didn't have to come here. I was going to bring it to you."

"That's okay, Anise." He moved closer.

"Let's focus on food," she said.

"But you look so pretty tonight." He placed his hands on her hips.

"Pete, no," She held the bowl in one hand and tried to peel off one of his hands with her other.

"Let her go." Carl spoke from the other side of the counter.

Pete turned.

"It's okay, Dad."

"Shit." Pete rubbed his hand over his face.

The door jingled and a policeman stood in the doorway with another behind him.

"Everyone doing alright in here?" the first officer said, an older man. "I saw the lights on."

"Yes, officer. This is my restaurant. I'm just having an after-hour party for family and friends."

"It didn't look too friendly. Can I see some ID?"

She pointed to the wall at her diploma and to the various permits. "Do those work?"

"We need some personal ID to verify it's you. Routine stuff, not to worry."

In her backroom, shushing Mandy who meowed, Anise found her purse and removed her wallet, hands shaking, while other items—compact, pens—hit the floor.

Returning, she saw that Pete had his hands in his jacket pocket and was staring at the floor, wavering, just waiting it out, familiar with interrogation.

Removing cards from her wallet, she handed them over to the policeman. He handed them back. "Do you have a liquor license?"

"No, but this isn't a public gathering. I'm not selling it. It's a private party."

"I understand, but that's sticky territory since it's being held in a public place. A fine would be steep."

"Bullshit," Pete said, quietly.

"Excuse me?" The second officer said, a young man, with clear skin and ready eyes.

"She's not doing anything wrong," Pete replied.

"Maybe, maybe not. But you're not helping her," the young cop said.

"More than you are," Pete replied, looking away.

"You're not looking to be taken in for insubordination, are you, young man?" the senior officer said.

"No, I sure as hell am not," he chuckled.

The older officer looked around the room, saw how everyone else was simply watching the situation, causing no disturbance. "What is your relationship?" he asked Anise, waving a finger back and forth between her and Pete.

"We're sweethearts," Pete stated.

"We're friends," Anise corrected, glaring at Pete.

"You know, I think it's time for me to leave," Pete said, and once on the other side of the counter, he pushed his way past the young officer, slamming his shoulder into him on the way to his bag.

At the booth, he grabbed his heavy bag and unzipped it. "Before I go, there's just one thing I want to give you, Anise."

The officers tuned in. Pete's tone had changed. They could read a twist in motives. They could read a shift, when something was about to go awry. They had been trained in stopping harm, in protecting the innocent, in obstructing evil.

The older one used words to create order: "Hold it right there. Put your hands up."

Pete wasn't listening. "I've wanted to give this to you for a while, Anise." And with that, Pete pulled something from his heavy bag.

"Put your hands up!" the young cop yelled.

"Pete, listen to him!" Anise screamed.

But Pete was mumbling something that no one heard, and as he swung around, the young police officer pointed with both hands and pulled his trigger.

Pete fell backward. A framed photo of himself flew out of his hand, high in the air before it hit the floor. It was a picture of another life. A life before war, a life where he wore hockey gear and a smile, where he was photogenic, low to the ice and holding his stick.

Cans of beer rolled out of his bag, one of them stopping at the foot of the young cop.

The older policeman immediately called for an ambulance. Anise rushed to Pete's aide. The students remained in their booth, dumbfounded. The three older men assessed the situation, knew not to move, computed the facts, talked quietly, would talk more later. But Bill had to say something. He rose from the booth, holding onto the table for balance.

"You just shot one of our own boys, son."

Anise kneeled over Pete, her hands on his face. "Pete. I'm so sorry. Please," she cried, "don't go. Don't leave me."

PART IV

RESCUES

The Last Taste

Anise woke late in the morning, Mandy licking from the bowl of Béchamel, which had oozed onto the blanket: a desecration. The white bread that had been given to her by the clerk at the food bank, that tasted good because of her cheese sauce, had rolled from her grip onto the floor. Out of sorts and heavy-headed from not bedding down properly, not washing and putting away food and supplies, her heart raced as she jolted up from her slouched position.

"I know how to clean up messes, thank you very much!" Anise spoke to her left, to her mother, on the verge of tears, as she viewed the sticky stain on the blanket. On all fours now, trying to rise, she lamented her loss. "How often do I get good cheese? And look what I go and do." For two minutes she mourned her loss, yelling at her mother and scolding herself as she cleaned up her dinner dishes, throwing a little fit as she would on occasion, banging her pot, slamming the cupboard door again and again so that Mandy ran to the door, clawing to escape. "Is it too much to ask? It is too much to—"

"What are you doing?"

Anise turned around and dropped her little stove,

isopropyl alcohol spilling onto the floor.

A tall man about fifty, wearing a short winter jacket and a scowl, loomed over her. Next to him, with wide eyes and a wide mouth, stood a younger woman, one hand on a cheek.

"What in the world are you doing?" The man asked again, throwing up his hands.

Anise opened her mouth but nothing came out.

"I think she's packing up. Isn't that it?" The woman had gentle eyes.

Anise nodded and kicked into gear. "Yes. Yes. It will just be a minute."

The two stood and watched until the woman touched the man's arm and ushered him out of the storeroom. Anise glanced at them as they left. She began to cry silently. Her vision blurry, she couldn't figure out what went where. Her hair hung over her right eye as her hairclip was off-center.

Stuffing all her belongings in her cart, she realized not all fit anymore since she had been using this room all year and had expanded her goods. Something had to give. She tried to shove her kitchenware down into her blanket, but there wasn't room, and it tumbled out and crashed to the floor. Flustered and whimpering, she removed her book, one blanket, and clothes. Still, it all wouldn't fit. Now what to leave behind? An extra pair of boots or cooking supplies? She threw the boots to the floor, set her cookware inside the big green garbage bag that contained it all, and squished the blanket onto the very top, inside the bag so it would stay dry.

Exiting as quietly as she could, she closed the door behind her. She dragged her cart off the landing and up the narrow driveway to the sidewalk, which had icy spots here and there. For the first time in a long time, she was lost and vulnerable. She glanced up the block, toward downtown. The women's shelter was on the way. Up the other way, it felt more manageable, though to what end?

It had been months and months since she had to find a place for the night. Suddenly startled by Mandy winding around her feet, she lost her footing and almost fell. Righting herself, she implored to Mandy. "What do we do?" She rubbed her face. "We'd better go." She pushed her cart away from the little building. Not toward downtown, but up Elmwood, toward Delaware Park. Yes. She'd curl into a corner of the casino. The hardest part would be dragging her cart through the park, over paths less paved, but she'd manage. She'd done it before.

"I'll manage!" Anise barked to her left. "Your days of comforting are long gone—and you're a fraud, a fraud!"

An older woman walked by just as she yelled and placed her hand on her heart, but Anise did not see her and continued to yell for half a block. As Anise looked at the windows of small eateries, she let her anger go. She wished she was presentable enough to step in and have a pastry, to sip some espresso, to be human. She wouldn't bother anyone; it was never her way. She'd keep to herself.

Mandy dashed past her. "Here, baby," Anise said. Mandy halted in her tracks and peered back at Anise. *Are you coming?*

They strode on, past the intersection of Elmwood and Forest. No street people loitered at the corner, and the psychiatric center was nestled behind its gates and trees. Mandy treaded quickly across the wide open crossing. Only now, crossing the street, did Anise feel self-conscious and vulnerable, a flash of who she used to be buzzing through her head. She yanked at her coat collar, an attempt to straighten it. She followed Mandy onto the pavement and felt better when she reached the shadows of trees and old homes. Mandy was leading the way to the casino, behind the art museum.

Behind the art museum was also a manmade lake. The lake was surrounded by three buildings: the museum, the historical society, which had tall columns like the museum, and the casino, which had smaller columns and terraces and was originally a boathouse where in the 1800s long-skirted ladies stood to gaze on the lake or canoed on the water with their men.

Anise wanted nothing to do with the lake as she pushed her cart over hard earth, avoiding patches of icy snow. Looking now at the casino, her home for the night, she pushed her cart near the structure and tucked it in a corner, next to the stairs. She walked up the steps to the many-windowed gathering hall. She peered in a window and was struck immediately that she had done this very thing before with George. This was one of the places they had discovered together. *Look in here,* she had said to him. *What do you think they did in here?* And she had told him how it reminded her *of that painting, the one made with the dots.*

This was their stage. Yes, she remembered now as she looked at the stretch of the walkway. An older couple had been at one end, and she and George had stepped into character.

"George! George, darling! Shall we go boating? Oh, you are a dear. Please, hear, help me with my shawl. I feel a chill!"

Anise was filled with pleasure and laughed and didn't want to leave that moment. Indeed, she tried to relive it as she spun and turned a corner of the casino and tripped over a man's outstretched legs. "Ugh!" She blurted. He had been sitting against the wall. Anise fell to the ground, catching herself with her palms, her legs on top of his.

"I'm sorry," Anise said and pushed her body off his, looking in his face as she rose, catching sight of a sickle-shaped scar under his eye.

"Hey, darlin', watch your step," The gray-bearded man said.

"Sorry, I, I—"

He reached in his bag and pulled out a bottle. "Need something to drown your sorrows?" He laughed, exposing a dark hole where teeth used to be.

Anise contracted and shook her head. He shrugged and took a swallow, capped it, and returned it to the bag.

Anise turned, shoved her gloved hand over her mouth and tried to run until she reached her cart, which she gripped and pushed up the path and over the hard earth until reaching the sidewalk.

For two blocks, Anise's vision was blurry and her sense of time and place swirled in her mind so that she had to stop and bend over her cart to keep from falling. She squeezed her eyes tight and breathed heavily until she felt a cool breeze on her cheek. She straightened up and got her bearings. Mandy was at her feet. She took a few breaths, looked around, remembered where she was, who she was. It would have to be the women's shelter after all.

It had been over a year since she had to sleep anywhere else. This she hated most of all, depending on people. Hives surfaced under her eyes as she thought of the bright lights, the rows of beds, the faces of the helpers who were only better off because they were weak and depended on others—husbands, employers, family. "Anyone can do that," she said, crossing the wide intersection again.

It would be an hour before she'd make it to the shelter, which was a good thing. She would feel like a prisoner once there. They had their rules, and she had hers.

About halfway there, she stopped in front of the library. It was a regular stop for her, her favorite place to be besides the home she had to leave. She dragged her cart up the path when she realized she couldn't take it in. This past year, she had been able to leave it in her room. As the months had ticked by, she had gotten accustomed to staying for longer hours in the library, longer periods without her cart. She had forgotten how she used to tuck it behind empty apartments and alleyways. She thought for a moment of leaving it in front, but she'd be warned to move it, or someone would take it away. She looked at the flyers on the glass door depicting workshops and readings. She just wanted the warmth and the quiet table and the books. No one would bother her. They'd leave her alone in her own world.

Turning from the doors, she pushed her cart to the sidewalk. A police car was at a light, and she lifted her chin and walked as if she were like anyone else, someplace to go, business to take care of.

Anise arrived at the women's and children shelter in the afternoon, earlier than she wanted. It was a new building, clean and with a courtyard for children to play. Anise felt too dirty to approach, but her choices were limited. "Stop giving me advice! I can handle this on my own, thank you very much!" She brushed away the nuisance at her left. Now, her face was spotted with hives. Pulling her cart to the door, it was difficult to keep the door open while entering with the cart, but she managed. She approached the window where the receptionist sat, secured behind walls against men who might enter, inquire or bully.

"Can I help you?"

"I need a place to stay for the night."

"Have you been here before?"

"A while back."

"What's your name?"

"Anise Kaufmann." It hurt to say.

"Oh yes, here you are. Two years ago, almost to the day." The woman peered at the details of her file. "How have you been?" Anise took this as a way for her to get information, not out of concern.

"I've been fine. I just want to stay a night and make some plans, if that is okay."

"That is definitely okay." She looked behind Anise at her cart. "Looks like you've got all your stuff with you. We're going to have to look through it and make sure there are no drugs, alcohol or weapons. It's just routine, honey."

Anise's faced blushed. She hated this part, her articles under bright lights, her old underwear examined.

Anise was offered entrance to the manor proper and

taken into the first room on the right.

"Just put your things on the table, dear."

With shaking, gloved hands, Anise untied the garbage bag and clutched her blanket, freshly washed the day before. Out came her cooking supplies, all inside a pot, except for the stove.

"I'll have to keep this locked up for you." The woman took Anise's knife, a small thing, meant only for paring.

"No, I can't let you take it. It belongs to me."

"I know it belongs to you, honey, but it is considered a dangerous item. We need to take safety precautions when women share the same room."

"Stay out of it!" Anise hollered and slapped the air next to her.

"It's the rules, ma'am. There's no reason to be so upset. We're just trying to help you."

"I won't hurt anyone. I need to cook."

"You don't have to cook while you are here, dear."

Anise began to fret and sniffle, taking back her things. She put her pot of supplies in the bag, and shoved the blanket on top. "Go jump back in the lake where you belong!" She wiped a tear off the tip of her nose and dragged her cart out the door of the room. When she got to the next door, she turned the knob but it was slippery in her glove.

"Trapped! Now what! No thanks to you!"

"Let me get that for you." The woman opened the door. Anise placed her in a difficult situation. Dangerous or violent people weren't allowed to cohabitate with others who needed safety most of all. Anise dragged her cart back into the neighborhood and into more places to be invisible.

Anise was glad to be rid of the shelter. She'd keep warm. She'd manage. Good thing she had her knife for protection.

"Oh! How could I forget you?"

Mandy was at her feet, meowing and meowing. "Let's

Made in the USA
Charleston, SC
04 June 2013

find a place."

They made their way back to Elmwood. There was a sharp, cold feeling in her left foot, and she knew immediately that meant a hole was in her boot. She paused in her step and thought of her pair that were left back in her room. Should she dare to sneak back in? No, no. She shook her head. They'd have locked it up good now. Probably replaced the lock. And she was hungry, too. She had a little food in her bag, but she had gotten so use to going to the food pantry as if it were the grocer, that she had lost some of her resourcefulness. She had gotten lazy.

New cafés had been popping up and closing down. And here was another, on the corner of West Utica. She looked at it from across the street, longingly. She wanted to be on the other side of the black iron gate, to sit on the other side of the stenciled glass. To have her profile shadowed and alive and warm, with a ceramic cup underneath and tiramisu on a small plate with a small, shiny fork placed alongside. She closed her eyes and watched herself reading a novel, at perfect peace, her heart beating as slowly as an athlete's heart at rest.

"It's that time," she said to Mandy. When things got desperate, when she smelled herself and needed coins to launder, or times like now, when she needed to feel human, she would pull her sign out of her bag, drape a scarf around her head, and beg.

But she couldn't do it here. It was right across from the café she wanted to enter. No, she'd have to walk two blocks away so that when she was ready, she could return, discard her desperation and walk through the café door like she owned the place.

Three dollars so far, and her wet foot was very cold. She would need ten for espresso and a piece of cake, and if they served her, a tip. Or maybe she could buy only cake with a glass of water. Either way, she didn't have enough,

and it had been an hour.

Mandy was not at her feet, but she knew she was on a side-street, looking for food, too.

Her back was cold, standing in one position. She decided to sit down, against the storefront that was for sale. The ground was drier against the façade, and she could place the cup in her lap, her sign against her chest. People would have to take an extra step to give her something, but she needed to rest and warm her back. She clutched her blanket and wrapped it around herself, lowering herself down.

Brisk strides flew by. So many strong legs she could see from under her shawl. A pair stopped and dropped a dollar in her cup.

"Thank you," she mumbled, too late, with a throaty voice. She closed her eyes and fell asleep.

Anise woke at dusk. Something stirred her; she realized it was thunder. Her cup was full of damp bills and coins. She counted through grogginess. Thirteen dollars and eleven cents total. Never had she been given so much money. Unfolding her legs was excruciating. Her feet had fallen asleep and the left, wet one she couldn't seem to wake up as she rubbed it. She forced herself to stand up, using her cart and the wall for balance. Wincing, she stayed bent over her cart for a minute. Mandy was nowhere to be seen, and it started raining hard. Some shops were closing up, and she wondered if she was too late. She figured no one would touch her cart for the few minutes it would take to walk up two blocks to see if the café was closed.

As she approached the iron gate, she couldn't see any customers sitting at the tables. A waitress was sweeping. She opened the gate, put her hand on the door handle and went inside.

"I'm sorry, we're closed," The woman behind the counter said.

"Closed?" Anise sniffed and touched her nose to her gloved hand.

"Yes. I'm sorry."

Anise stood there, not wanting to leave the warmth, the lovely space.

The sweeping waitress shot a look to the woman behind the counter.

"Oh, I see." But still Anise remained.

The woman behind the counter was around thirty and thin and pretty, her dark hair tied back in a sleek, small ponytail. Her stomach was soft though, under her apron, probably from children. She seemed to look at Anise with pity and stopped wiping the counter.

"How about some muffins? I can't sell these tomorrow, so you are welcome to take them with you." She bagged them as she spoke.

"No, thank you." Anise shuffled closer to the long glass case between them and peered in, her face alight from the tasteful lamps that hung down from the ceiling. The woman watched as Anise's eyes sparkled at the beautiful pastries and cakes.

"Do you make the marzipan yourself?" Anise looked up for a moment then continued inspecting.

"Yes, yes I do." She looked over to the waitress, flashing a discreet and quick gaze of disbelief.

"It's not almond paste? Not from a can?"

"No, no. It's a recipe I learned in culinary school."

Anise nodded.

"And the tiramisu? Is it made with Marsala?"

"Well, no, I use Kahlua." The woman wiped her hands on her apron, concern in her brow.

"I see." Anise continued to scan the case, exhaling her disappointment. "Marsala is traditional. But I understand."

The waitress swept slowly and watched.

"Your cannoli are beautiful."

The woman lit up. "I use mascarpone cheese in

addition to ricotta. And Grand Marnier instead of vanilla."

"Oh, very nice!" Anise walked further down the case. "But they really should be filled to order, or the shells will soften."

The woman furrowed her brow, concentrating on something. "How about trying my pasticiotti. It's my specialty. I'd love to know what you think."

Anise met her eyes. "Do you have almond?"

"Yes, I do. It's my favorite," she said.

"Mine, too," said Anise, her fingers resting on the edge of the glass.

"Why don't you sit down and I'll bring it to you. It will take us some time to clean up."

The waitress held the broom and watched, mouth open, as Anise made her way to the window. Sitting down, Anise exhaled and angled her feet to the heat that pumped through the vent from the wall. She looked through the glass and the rain at Blue Mountain Coffee across the street. "Could I have coffee, too?" Anise spoke across the room, her voice clear.

"Espresso?" asked the woman, reaching for a fork.

"That would be lovely." Anise removed her gloves, one finger at a time, setting them neatly on the table. She straightened her back and waited.

Anise drank her last sip of espresso and tucked all but a dollar and the change next to the empty plate. She was warm now, except for the toes on her left foot, which stung. She pushed in her chair and shuffled to the bathroom. There, she wished she could wash her body but couldn't do it because not only could she be caught, it would also ruin the moment. Instead, she grabbed paper towels and squeezed hand soap on them, tucking them into her pocket for later. She grabbed more paper towels to shove into her boots later on, too.

She thanked the pastry chef and nodded to the waitress

who flitted out the door. Anise pulled on her gloves that now felt cold and damp, and she walked out onto the street.

The sight of her cart struck her with fear. She had completely forgotten she had left it there. Before she fell asleep, the plan had been to tuck it away. But there it was, and the sight of it made her walk quicker. Mandy was not around, and she worried because it had been a year for Mandy, too, of having the same place to stay. Mandy may have thought she abandoned her.

She checked her cart; everything seemed in order. Grabbing the handle, she angled it and made her way down Elmwood until she located a narrow driveway between two buildings. "Yes, that's right. I remember now." She had been here a number of times. A driveway that led to a small parking area for employees. Wooden fences in disrepair. A good spot to hide in, a prime spot. She wheeled slowly in case anyone else was back there. It had happened more than once, and it could be good or bad, someone to talk to or someone to hurt you. Most people were harmless, but the druggies were the worst because they were desperate. They were easy to spot, with their quick movements and needy look in their eyes.

All was quiet in the small lot except for the rain dripping from the eaves. Under a wide overhang next to a building, it was dry. She tucked her cart next to it and sat on the ground. Her toes had no feeling, and she wasn't sure what to do about that. She might have to ask for help at the shelter after all, just to get dry socks and new boots. She closed her eyes and swallowed in the pain of dependency.

In the meantime, she thought she could warm her foot and get comfortable in her blanket. She stood up and pulled out the blanket and another set of mismatched socks. Rain dripped down all around her, but she was untouched, so she was grateful for her spot.

There was a changing then, in the pattern of the rain,

something odd that she couldn't quite make out, a picking up of speed, a rush of air. She looked up, trying to detect the change, then she gasped when the rush was two men, one with a sunken mouth and one with scabs on his face.

"Here's somethin'," Sunken Mouth said to Scabs.

"Well, let's see what she's got." Scabs dug in her cart and threw the handmade stove to the ground, sending the dented cans rolling away. His eyelids twitched again and again.

"Where's your stash?" Sunken Mouth grabbed her by her coat collar so his face was right in hers.

"Lookie here." Scabs pulled the damp sign from the dry bag.

"Where the fuck is your money, lady!" Sunken mouth punched her in the face and jammed his hands in her coat pockets, pulling out a dollar and eleven cents. "That's it? That's the fuck it?" He smacked her body against the building three times, her head smashing the old red bricks. She fell to the ground and Scabs kicked her in the back as she fell. "Don't waste our time, bitch!"

****

Anise could hear voices, but she couldn't see, even though her eyes were open—at least, she thought they were open. Her head was bandaged and so was her side. Tubes came out of her side, her vagina, and one was taped to her arm that led to a bottle hanging from an aluminum pole. The most important tube was inserted into her mouth and down her windpipe and was connected to a ventilator.

Anise's heart beat slower than it ever had, slower than anyone's in the hospital that day. A nurse came in the room but Anise was unaware. The nurse took her vitals, marked them on the paper. She pulled back the sheet and examined the tube coming from her side. She then looked at her left foot, the toes green. She looked at the readings

on the ventilator and wrote on her clipboard.

Anise didn't know where she was, but more than that, she didn't try to think of where she was. Her thoughts were operating on another plane—maybe not thoughts at all.

She didn't think about her cart, which was tipped over behind a building, a layer of snow covering the spilt contents that mattered to no one, that would be thrown out, the item at the very bottom of the cart, an old cookbook.

She didn't think of Mandy either, who had found the cart and slept on the blanket during the night but who was now perched on a concrete window ledge one building over, eyes narrowed to slits.

The nurse left.

The temperature in the room dropped.

For a few seconds, Anise's heart sped up, as it had always done these past years at times like this, but it couldn't fight what was to be, and it slowed back down.

A breeze jostled the liquid hanging on the pole.

A paper couldn't be signed. No one to put her out of her suffering, a ward of the state—Anise, pushed on her side and propped with a rolled-up towel to curb the spreading of bed sores. Visited by no one. No longer human.

A mother never wants her child to suffer. She will go to great lengths to keep it from happening. And with the last winds Laura would ever muster on this earth, she first pushed a button, turning off the ventilator alarm. Then in the stillness of the room, except for the pumping of the oxygenated air, she used the last of her cold wind and yanked the tube from Anise's mouth, causing quiet coughs, then gasps, and fifteen minutes later, silence. And during that time, Anise let her thoughts take her away.

****

Anise stood in her old living room on Meridian, looking around at the furniture, one last time. It had been a difficult year. Anise hadn't bounced back from Pete's death, and she never would.

After he was shot and rushed to the hospital, and after Bill and Anise searched his records and for his family and made sure he was buried with honors, Anise closed up shop. Even if she hadn't had a breakdown, even if she hadn't blamed herself for his death, she would have had no choice but to close up. Her expenses had exceeded her income that last month, and then her business had all but stopped completely after the story had run in the papers and on TV. No one wanted to buy a sticky bun where blood had spilled.

She had to move in with her dad, which was a nice way to mourn, if you had to mourn, but it was one time too many. One month into her stay in her old room, she walked into the living room one evening, ready to speak, ready to sit with her dad over coffee, and he was dead on the sofa. Nothing tragic, nothing painful, just a stopping of the heart. There he lay, his head tilted into his curled fingers, the TV going, his eyes closed. He had dozed during one of his favorite shows and never woke up. Anise stood there with two cups, both with cream and sugar, in the middle of saying, "Well, it isn't the best coffee, but it's—" And there he lay, like a child, slumber overtaking him, and perhaps feeling content that Anise was back in her room. He was ready to relax.

Standing there, she had heard something rattling, rattling, and realized it was the cups and saucers she was holding. Through blurry eyes, she set them on the coffee table, proud of herself for a split second for keeping them from spilling.

On her knees, she found herself again looking into the face of a dead man. Collapsing on his chest, she bawled into the flannel, regretting that even for the short time they lived together again, she hadn't given him time.

And here she stood in her living room, one more year having passed, another man dead and gone. Things had to be done, but she wanted to hide away, to escape the drowning feeling. Taxes needed to be paid, and she had no money. Though her dad had created a little filing system made out of manila folders (she had shown him how, way back), some of which still had her curly cursive on the tabs, faded—Electric, Phone—she hadn't faced the contents and had let the notices pile up. Her electricity had been shut off last month; she was using candles at night, eating dry food. Her father had the smallest of life insurance policies, and she used it to pay for his funeral, burying him right next to her mother, as planned.

She had to go, to just walk away. The closing of her business had been hard enough. Midway through cleaning and removing things from the premises, she just stopped. Unplugging her bakery sign, she had let the cord hang. Her diploma was left on the wall. She simply picked up her purse, stopped herself from locking the door, and walked across the city in her sandals to her dad's house where she knocked and ambled to her room without saying a word. As the days crawled by, she grieved in a state of suspension, passing her father in the hall on her way to the bathroom in a slow haze. He'd knock lightly and leave a plate at her door. Her room had been left the same, Adam Ant posters over her bed, like her mother's items, still there. Time passed, and she hadn't. People passed, and she remained, right back where she started.

Anise now stood in the living room, wearing extra layers of clothes and a backpack from high school she had found in her closet. Anise was broken, so that she actually felt a crack in her body—she could see it, too. She traced it sometimes with her finger, at night, alone in her old bedroom. It began at her heart, at the breast, a line, the lightest of lines, pale, like meringue. The line made its way down, past her navel, down one thigh, and ended in a

bulging, blue vein in her calf—the vein that had formed from years of standing, of baking for people whom she'd never talk to. Sometimes, she'd stare at the vein, almost sure it would burst, at which point she'd cover it quick with her blanket and fall asleep with the white ceiling light on.

Now, in the living room, she found it very hard to make her move. Her plan was to take the fifty dollars she had and to take a bus, to keep taking buses to the end of the line, wherever that was, some city, some state, somewhere. She could think and sleep on the buses as they made their many stops. Life could be a nonstop ride. She'd make do. She was resourceful. But standing there, she couldn't bring herself to open the door and go. The weight of her pointlessness felt so heavy that she folded into the sofa and sobbed into the cushions.

She heard a knock on the side of the house, on the screen door. That was odd because only she and her dad used the side door. Many people were after her right then, debt collectors—taxes, water, everything. She had been keeping the curtains closed, the front door locked, even the screen door. Maybe they decided to try the side. Had she locked the side door after taking garbage to someone else's can that evening? She wasn't sure! Tiptoeing to the kitchen, she heard the screen door open. A loud knock on the door startled her, and her heart thudded, so much so that she saw her shirt vibrate. She placed her hand on it, afraid that somehow it would alert the intruder.

The knocking stopped, and she heard the doorknob turn. She hadn't locked it! At the kitchen door, at the same time she heard steps, she quietly turned the lock tight on the gold-colored knob. Someone was on the other side of the door. Then a loud knock that caused Anise to squeal.

"Anise? Anise, are you there?"

The voice was strange, yet familiar. Deep, but there was something there that rang from her childhood.

"Yes?" she braved.

"Well, are you going to open up?" he asked.

Anise leaned into the door, squeezed her eyes shut. Her legs began to give. She couldn't be wrong. If she were to open the door, if anyone else should be there, she wouldn't make it another day. She was afraid though. Afraid of letting this moment go. Afraid of losing someone else. Maybe she'd just pretend that it was him and never open the door. Maybe she'd lean on the door forever. She wouldn't have to move from this spot. She could just remain.

"Anise?"

"George?" A tear rolled down her cheek. "Is it you?"

"Open the door, you goof. How long are you going to keep me waiting?"

Ever so slowly, she opened the door. There he stood, and there she stood, shaking her head and crying. "Oh, George. It's you."

"Yes, it's me. Your phone isn't working. Did you know that? Aren't you going to ask me in?"

Anise started laughing. She was alive. She was human. George was there, and already he was making it all right. Just the sight and sound of him, just George talking to Anise, picking right up where they left off. "Please, darling," she said in affection, forcing her tears far, far away, "Come in." And she stepped aside and swept her arm in a big, theatrical arc for him to enter.

ABOUT THE AUTHOR

Thea Swanson is an American author of literary fiction. Her short stories have been published in numerous literary journals. She received an MFA in Writing from Pacific University in 2007 and has taught creative writing, English, and film and literature courses to middle-schoolers, high-schoolers, and college students. Swanson currently runs a manuscript editing boutique at mssediting.com and lives near Seattle with her husband and three children. *The Curious Solitude of Anise* is her first novel.